MEDIAPOLIS PUBLIC LIBRARY
128 N. ORCHARD ST.
MEDIAPOLIS, IA 52637

NATIONAL BURDEN

8/19

Help us Rate this book...
Put your initials on the
Left side and your rating
on the right side.
1 = Didn't care for
2 = It was O.K.
3 = It was <u>great</u>

	DATE DUE		
AUG 2 6 2019			
DEC 0 6 2019			
DEC 1 8 2019			

		Rating
MRH	1 2 ③
	1 2 3
	1 2 3
	1 2 3
	1 2 3
	1 2 3
	1 2 3
	1 2 3
	1 2 3
	1 2 :
	1 2 :
	1 2 :
	1 2 :
	1 2 3
	1 2 3

D1113480

PRINTED IN U.S.A.

NATIONAL
BURDEN

Book 5 of the Corps Justice Series

C. G. COOPER

ISBN: 1517207983
ISBN-13: 9781517207984

Get a **FREE** copy of any *Corps Justice* novel by signing up to my **New Release Mailing List.**

Warning: This story is intended for mature audiences and contains profanity and violence.

A huge thanks to my Beta Readers. You guys are amazing!
To our amazing troops serving all over the world, thank you
for your bravery and service.
Semper Fidelis

CHAPTER 1

The resort was new. In fact, it wasn't even open to the public yet. Mexican laborers could still be heard pounding away, rushing to finish before the hoped-for Spring Break rush.

He was staying with an old friend, a buddy who'd recently taken a cruel turn, constantly hounding him, concocting new schemes, pushing him further than before. Their stay was a favor from a new contact, a wealthy donor who happened to be a developer that owned properties all over coastal Mexico and wanted to attract high-end clientele from the States. They wouldn't be bothered in the elegantly appointed private penthouse on the edge of the resort.

It was probably only seventy degrees, but to the man sitting in the white plastic chair, the kind that were supposed to be high-end but felt like they would break with slightest movement, the temperature felt stifling. His senses were on edge, catching the whir of the air conditioning, the flip of the overhead fan, the light step of his captor.

"You failed."

1

Santos Lockwood squirmed in his seat, the fabric of his patterned board shorts suddenly clinging to his legs. "It's not my fault. I tried to keep my job and do what you planned."

The man at the window turned, casting a shadow across his perfectly tanned face. "I can understand how the last president's departure was not your fault, but I can't understand why you couldn't make yourself useful to Zimmer."

Lockwood looked up at his old friend, the annoyingly good-looking, always coifed Republican congressman from Florida Antonio McKnight. "Come on, Tony. It happens every time a new administration comes in. Out with the old, in with the new. It was bound to happen sometime." He added a nervous chuckle, hoping his friend would lighten up.

Tony McKnight put a hand on his trim stomach and closed his eyes. "Yes, that happens when there's a normal turnover, but Zimmer took over abruptly when your old boss abdicated the throne. From what I hear, Zimmer hasn't cleaned house, so don't feed me your line of bullshit. I've bailed you out more than once, Santos." McKnight's steel blue eyes flared open. It felt to Lockwood like they were burning a hole in his forehead. "I got you that fucking job! You've always been a fuckup, even in college. If it wasn't for me you wouldn't have made it out of Florida State with a diploma." As quickly as his temper burst, it melted away with the tropical air, blown by the seventy degree breeze whirring the scent of the newly constructed condo. "Now, tell me why I should even listen to you."

Lockwood gritted his crooked teeth. He'd always played second fiddle to his playboy friend, but he wasn't without his worth. Lockwood thought back to the nights spent tracking down his freshman roommate, finally finding him stumbling home from yet another girl's dorm room as the sun peaked over the horizon. Nursing him back to health. Dragging him to class. He'd been the one to ensure McKnight's diploma, not the other way around.

McKnight's moves and cunning improved with age. He was always hungry and it eventually landed him a republican congressional seat in Miami. Lockwood was the liberal, but their half Hispanic heritage, and their history, always pulled them together.

"I don't know what to say. I...tell me what you want me to say."

Congressman McKnight shook his head. "Wrong answer, Santos." A shrill whistle from McKnight's lips caused a side door to open. Two deeply tanned Mexicans entered the room, faces placidly menacing, almost bored. "You remember my cousins, Felix and Miguel."

The blood drained from Lockwood's face. "What are they doing here?"

Antonio McKnight flashed the brilliant smile that had captured many a young girl's heart and now captivated much of conservative America. Like a diamond expertly crafted by an aged jeweler, Tony looked confident, composed, and powerful with his perfectly tailored clothes and talk. Half white and half Hispanic, a man trapped between both worlds, plagued by his past yet using it to propel him forward. Rather than wallowing in his history, McKnight used it to feed his increasing hunger for power. Insatiable.

He'd seen the stare from the unmarried congressman before. Predatory. To Lockwood it looked more like a wolf preparing to strike, stalking its prey. McKnight nodded to the two men, supposedly his cousins, but Santos Lockwood knew differently. Hired thugs. Murderers.

Before he could react, they had his arms pinned to the glass table. "Let me go!" he yelled, panicking, a trickle of pee turning into a stream running down his leg.

Neither man flinched, faces remaining expressionless. McKnight moved to the wet bar. "Now, the way I see it, normally there's a time for forgiveness and a time for lessons. This may be a time for both."

Sweat poured from Lockwood's gray forehead. "Please, Tony. Please don't kill me." He knew what his old pal was capable of. The friendly facade that the public knew masked a ruthless personality, chiseled and hammered into a vessel of power. His twisted youth had turned him into a duplicitous monster, Dr. Jekyll and Mr. Hyde.

McKnight laughed, turning back to the trio, now holding a long filet knife in his right hand. "If I wanted to kill you, you'd already be dead." He admired the blade, caressing its length with his index finger. "You had a very simple job. Stay close to the President. Did you do that? No."

"But—"

"Here's what's going to happen. I'm going to give you one last shot, and only because I love you like a brother and your mom was always nice to me. But if you fail me this time, if you once again forget everything I've done for you and for your family…" The wicked grin on McKnight's face left little doubt in Santos Lockwood's mind. What had happened to the affable kid he'd met that first sunny day of school in Tallahassee?

Lockwood's shoulders slumped and his chin dropped to his chest. "Tell me what you want me to do."

"I'll tell you that later," Lockwood's head snapped up at the feel of another grip on his hand. It was McKnight's. "Right now, I need to give you an excuse and a lesson."

Without warning, the razor sharp knife bit into Lockwood's fingers, sawing with excruciating accuracy. The smile never left the congressman's face. Even as his friend screamed, he sliced away, one finger gone already, blood spraying unceremoniously across the table, accompanied by the wild cackle of his friend.

CHAPTER 2

STOKES SECURITY INTERNATIONAL (SSI) HEADQUARTERS,
CAMP SPARTAN, ARRINGTON, TN
9:29 A.M., FEBRUARY 27TH

The majority owner of Stokes Security International, Calvin Stokes, Jr., adjusted himself in the leather desk chair, realizing his butt had gone numb. He'd been at it since 4:30 a.m., all thanks to the grief his cousin Travis Haden, SSI's CEO and a former SEAL, had given him a week before for not staying on top of his administrative duties.

Cal hated anything that had the word *admin* in it. The Marine infantryman in him wanted to be out at the range, or in the live fire house, honing his skills. He felt those skills melting away as he perused yet another profit & loss statement.

He knew it was pointless thinking about it. February had been one of the coldest in Tennessee history, and SSI had closed all non-essential facilities for three days running. Being cooped up in an office grated on his every nerve as he sat behind his father's old desk.

Cal glanced at the picture of him and his father, both wearing matching orange University of Virginia shirts. It was taken on Cal's first day at U.Va right after they'd unpacked everything in his new Humphrey's Dorm room. He loved the picture for many reasons, but mostly because of how his father had been that day. The former Marine colonel wasn't known for being overly emotional, but on that day, Calvin Stokes, Sr. had cried, more out of pride than of sorrow, for his son's accomplishments.

If he looked closely at the photo, Cal could see the tinge of red in his father's eyes. He missed his parents deeply and kept their memory close at hand.

"Don't tell me *you* liked all this paperwork, Dad."

His father, though an officer, was a grunt as well, leading Marines for almost twenty years. There wasn't much the former Marine Staff Sergeant wouldn't have done to see his father one more time.

As he reached for another folder, his office door opened. Former Marine Master Sergeant Willy Trent, a beast of a man just shy of a hulking seven feet, poked his head in. "You decent?"

Cal smiled. "Come on in, Top. I was getting ready to take a break."

Trent stepped into the office and whistled when he saw the thick stacks of reports on his friend's desk. "What's all this?"

"Some stuff Trav wants me to get familiar with. I guess I've been putting it off long enough."

MSgt Trent's laugh came straight from his belly. He pointed a finger at Cal. "They finally got you, Cal. They're turning you into a rear echelon motherfucker."

Cal's eyes narrowed as he gave his friend the finger. "Fuck you, Top." He said it with a smile, and stood up from his desk.

"You wanna get a couple rounds in? I'll tie one arm behind my back," asked Trent.

Cal Stokes could take down most men in hand-to-hand combat, but he'd never bested Trent on the mats. They sparred regularly, always with the same outcome: the black Marine with the NFL lineman's physique won.

"Why not? This stuff can wait."

An hour and five submissions later, Cal was dripping in sweat. He'd almost locked Trent in an arm bar once, but the crafty Marine had slipped out of it with practiced ease. "I'm spent. Wanna grab an early lunch?"

MSgt Trent wiped his obsidian brow with a towel. "Yeah. How about we call up a couple of the boys and have them join us?"

One of the secrets to SSI's success was the tight knit relationships of its men. Even a lot of the guys in tech and development came from the military, led by the genius world class hacker and Vice President of R&D Neil Patel. They were the best of the best, patriots to the core. They stayed because they were well cared for and because of the feeling of family, first instilled by Cal's father, and now carried on by him and his cousin. There wasn't a thing any of SSI's leaders would ask their men to do that they hadn't done themselves. Leadership by example.

Cal stomped the snow from his boots before stepping into the cafeteria. It was one of many modern, yet Spartan facilities built on the 2,000-odd acre SSI campus. There was The Lodge, the VIP quarters with the rustic log cabin facade, its interior spanning thousands of square feet. The headquarters and support buildings were clustered in a simple grid, allowing each division privacy, much like military regiments and battalions. Again, yet another piece of Col. Stokes's vision.

The chow hall was nearly empty, most employees opting to stay home. Laughter directed Cal and Trent to their friends. A slightly portly man with glasses, Dr. Alvin Higgins, was telling a story to the rest of the bunch. Dr. Higgins was SSI's in-house shrink and expert interrogator. Originally on loan from the CIA, Higgins was now a permanent fixture at SSI. He looked more like an English professor, but he'd proven himself time after time with SSI's operators. They knew him and trusted him completely.

The men at the table turned as the two Marines approached.

"Would you look at what the snow blew in," said a squat, almost burly man with his beard neatly tied in twin braids.

"Shouldn't you be somewhere closer to the equator, Gaucho?" asked MSgt Trent. "The last time you saw snow you almost froze your little Mexican ass off."

"Hey, Top, can you blame me?"

Trent walked up behind Gaucho and picked him up in a bear hug. The tough Hispanic squirmed as the others laughed. The Marine and former Delta soldier were relentless in their ribbing. Cal often wondered where other than in the military, or at SSI, two men with such different backgrounds could become best friends.

There were three others at the table. Neil Patel was SSI's head of technology and development. The Indian-American was the smartest man most of them had ever met. He kept SSI at the forefront of the world's technological advances while also bringing in millions of dollars from licensing newly developed inventions. Always the most stylish man in the room, today Neil had opted for a pink and aqua checkered shirt and a pair of white pants. Not exactly what you might call appropriate for the weather, but Neil wasn't a field guy.

The other man sitting next to Neil was SSI's head of Internal Security. Todd Dunn was a former Army Ranger and Travis Haden's right hand. The brawny yet brainy sentinel sat smiling, but didn't say much.

The last man pointed to the seat next to him, motioning Cal over. Daniel Briggs kept his shoulder length blonde hair in a neat pony tail. The former Marine sniper was to Cal Stokes what Dunn was to SSI's CEO. If Cal went anywhere, Daniel was with him. Part bodyguard, part advisor, part guardian angel, Daniel had become one of Cal's closest friends despite their short acquaintance. There had been more than one occasion where the dead calm sniper the men called Snake Eyes had saved Cal's life.

Everyone took their seats as Cal joined Trent to grab some food. As the unofficial head of food services, Trent inspected the line with a practiced eye. A new line cook looked on nervously. "Looks good today, Vince," said Trent.

"Thanks, Master Sergeant. I used the bread pudding recipe you showed me. I think it turned out pretty good."

Trent took a spoonful of the bread pudding in his mouth, chewing slowly. "Not bad. Not bad at all."

The line cook smiled proudly.

As he took his seat, Cal asked, "Where's Travis?"

Dunn spoke up for the first time. "He and The Hammer flew to D.C."

The Hammer was SSI's sole female employee, Marge Haines. As the company's lead attorney, Haines had attained the moniker by destroying opposition in and out of the courtroom, as well as on the training mats. Haines was not only brilliant and beautiful; she was also a black belt in three martial arts disciplines. She could go toe-to-toe with the best that SSI had.

Cal's eyebrow rose. "He didn't tell me about that. What's up?"

"President Zimmer wanted to talk to him about something," said Dunn.

"And you didn't go with him?"

The question obviously struck a nerve, as the normally unflappable Dunn scowled slightly. "He said he wanted me to keep an eye on things here."

Cal let it go, not wanting to annoy Dunn further. The group spent the rest of their meal listening to more new tales from Dr. Higgins's time with the Agency.

CHAPTER 3

The normal buzz of activity vibrated around them as they made their way to the heart of the American government. There seemed to be an added level of tension thrown into the mix. A huff here or a withdrawn look there. The White House staff looked tired. Exhausted, actually.

It shouldn't have been a surprise what with the recent upheaval within the presidency. Anytime you change leadership, and especially if the change involved scandalous tidings, there's sure to be more than enough bedlam to go around.

Travis Haden, attired in a gray suit, sans tie, stepped into the Oval Office, Marge Haines on his heels. "I'm sorry we're late, Mr. President. The weather almost kept us from getting here."

President Brandon Zimmer, a Democrat from Massachusetts, now sporting a line of gray hair he hadn't had months before, stepped from behind his desk. In his mid-thirties, the bachelor who had become president overnight was considered by the world as one of the newest most eligible. With near movie star good looks and a political pedigree that spanned back decades, Zimmer reminded many of Jack Kennedy. "Come on, Trav, you know you can call still call me Brandon."

Their handshake turned into a brotherly embrace. "What can I say, I'm a little awed by your new digs."

Zimmer rolled his eyes, knowing the former SEAL well. Not much awed Travis Haden, except maybe the woman standing next to him. "Ms. Haines, it's a pleasure to see you again."

"Thank you, Mr. President."

"Not you too!" The President laughed, and directed them to the couches in front of the roaring fireplace. They exchanged pleasantries as they got situated. Now up to speed, Zimmer said, "I'll bet you're wondering why I asked you to come."

Travis and Marge nodded, both having made certain assumptions on the flight over. Travis knew his friend was in a tight spot, having landed the job in the craziest way anyone could remember.

"First, and I'm begging this time, please call me Brandon. I get enough ass-kissing around here. I thought it was bad when I was a lowly congressman." Zimmer exhaled. He looked drained, older. Travis couldn't imagine being thrust into the spotlight the way Zimmer had. In the span of a few months, Congressman Zimmer won his father's seat in the Senate, followed shortly by his appointment as vice president when the former VP was assassinated. As if that weren't enough, not weeks later, his predecessor, the first African American president, resigned in a televised address to the nation, handing the reins to his vice president. To say

Zimmer had been shocked would've been the understatement of the millennium.

"Second, I need your honest opinion."

"You know us, we're happy to help." Travis waited for Zimmer, who seemed to be lost in thought. After a moment, his eyes refocused. The President ran a hand through his perfectly styled hair, disheveling it slightly.

"I hesitated calling you. I mean, SSI has done more than its fair share of heavy lifting for me and for this country..." Again, the distant gaze.

"You're not going to offend us, Brandon. Why don't you just tell us what's going on."

Zimmer exhaled. "I remember as a kid, when my third grade teacher asked us what we wanted to be when we grew up, I said I wanted to be President of the United States. That sounds silly now."

"Seems to me that you got what you wanted," offered Travis, wondering where his friend was going with his nostalgic meandering. Worry crept into Travis's chest, something that rarely happened. Two years before he wouldn't have cared a bit for a democratic politician, but SSI had forged a lasting relationship with the man who was now the leader of the free world. Catastrophe and calamity had changed Brandon Zimmer. Once a vain and cocky career bureaucrat, Zimmer's eyes had opened to the realities of the world.

"I'm not so sure about that."

Silence in the room. Marge coughed into her hand, causing the men to swivel their heads.

"No offense, Mr. President, but like it or not, you earned this. Call it being in the right place at the right time, or dumb luck, but you're still the president. Now, I'm sure Travis will agree with me when I say that the two of us, along with the rest of Stokes Security International, are with you, and are ready to help in any way we can."

The President nodded, sitting a little straighter at the honest talk from the tough lawyer. "You're right, of course. I'm sorry if I'm acting a little down in the mouth. It's not that I'm not grateful, but I'm surrounded by the old president's staff. I've made a little headway to build my own inner circle while trying not to step on people who had the rug ripped out from under them. You wouldn't believe what this has done to morale around here. Let's start with my second request. I need your honest opinion."

An hour later, Travis and Marge left the Oval Office, three cabinet members taking their place as they went. Neither said a word as they passed through security or even on the cab ride to their hotel. There was plenty to be said. The level of transparency shown by the President had both impressed and shocked the SSI leaders. Their minds replayed the exchange in vivid detail, extracting bits and filing them away.

After a painfully slow drive through snow-clogged streets, they made it to their hotel and stepped into one of their adjoining rooms.

Travis closed the door and set his overnight bag on the floor. "What do you think?"

Marge laughed, a hint of hysteria at the edges of it. "Are you kidding? I don't know what you see in the guy. Seems like a—"

"Stop. I know what you're going to say, and while I appreciate your dissection of Zimmer's attitude, I'd prefer to focus on what he asked us about."

It looked like Marge was going to bark back. She wanted to. "Okay. But I need to say that he should look in the mirror and grow a pair. He's the President of the United States for God's sake!"

Travis couldn't disagree. The depth of Zimmer's melancholy had surprised him. He knew Brandon Zimmer as an outgoing, confident man. Sure, he'd had a few bumps along the way, but he always came out stronger on the other side.

"What do you think about his question?"

Haines's frown disappeared, replaced slowly by a sarcastic grin. "You're serious? Tell me you're not considering it."

Travis shrugged. "I can't say it isn't tempting. There are obvious benefits for the company, not to mention the good it could do."

"I think you should talk to Cal first. You know he's not going to like it."

A laugh escaped Travis's lips. "You've got that right. I don't want to do it over the phone, though." He pulled his cell out of his suit pocket. "Let me see if I can find us a flight home."

CHAPTER 4

The massive building was empty. Senators and congressman were either hunkered down in their Capitol digs or already safely in their home states. Snow caked every window, casting a gray tint into hallways. A lone janitor, busy buffing the gleaming floor, nodded to Senator Milton Southgate as he walked by.

Sen. Southgate was a twenty year pillar in the Senate. As Senate Majority Leader, Southgate ruled with a firm hand. Bookish in appearance, with thick glasses that had changed little since his first term, Milton Southgate led an extremely regimented life. After losing his wife years before, his obsessive tendencies intensified. For example, his aides knew to have sticky rollers on hand should a stray piece of lint appear on the senator's well-worn suit. If they didn't, well, it was best not to find out.

No one would necessarily call the senator a miser, but Southgate was very particular on a great number of things, perhaps the most important being timeliness. He had fired more than his share of staff for failing to be on time. Being one minute late was a crime in the Senate Majority Leader's office.

His meeting was the reason he was the sole senator in the building during the snowstorm that had necessitated an emergency shutdown of the entire District of Columbia. Southgate had made an appointment and he meant to keep it. Blizzard be damned.

Fully fifteen minutes early, Sen. Milton Southgate entered the reserved conference room. A patient man despite his compulsions, Southgate took a seat at the polished table, clasping his hands across his stomach.

Precisely at 4:30 p.m., Congressman Antonio McKnight entered the room. He was alone. This surprised Southgate. The young Republican was known for his entourage. *This should be interesting*, thought the Democrat from Arizona. He'd never met McKnight in person, but like everyone in Washington, he'd seen plenty of the handsome man on television.

"Senator Southgate, thank you so much for seeing me." McKnight walked around the conference table to shake hands.

"You said it was important."

McKnight nodded, taking a seat at the head of the table. *He thinks he belongs in that chair*, Southgate mused. The senior senator had chosen a neutral chair in the middle of the ten person table.

Exhaling dramatically, McKnight smiled. "Quite an interesting couple of months, wouldn't you say?"

Southgate wasn't going to give the upstart an inch. He'd learned long ago that it was better to sit and listen. Instead of answering, he nodded.

"I can only imagine what was going through your head when you heard about the President resigning. Were you there?" asked McKnight.

"I was not."

"I was in Miami. I'm still in shock."

Again, a non-committal nod from Southgate. There was silence as the congressman gathered his thoughts.

Southgate leaned forward an inch, looking over his glasses like a school teacher. "May I call you Antonio?"

"Call me Tony."

"Antonio, I don't mean to be inhospitable, but I drove through a snowstorm to meet you. Maybe we could get to the point." It wasn't said condescendingly. In fact, it was just the opposite, like a high school teacher patiently showing his student how to get a handle on calculus.

"You're right. I'm sorry. Like I said, I can only imagine how much upheaval the President's resignation has caused. My party took it in the teeth when Nixon left, leaving Ford to pick up the pieces." McKnight paused again, looking down at his hands. "Now, I know we're on opposite sides of the aisle, but I think we can both agree that Zimmer, excuse me, President Zimmer, while likable, may not be the best fit to lead this country."

Southgate's eyes narrowed. "Why should I care what you think? You're talking about the President of the United States, an upstanding member of my party."

McKnight's hands upturned in front of him. "Come on, Senator, you probably didn't like it when a first-term congressman took over a very influential seat in the Senate. Now he's President? You can't tell me that doesn't piss you off."

"Once again, I fail to see why I should sit and listen to your opinion. Then Congressman Zimmer won his father's vacated seat honestly and overwhelmingly. His appointment to vice president was endorsed by both parties. He didn't choose to be president. We all saw the look on his face at the news conference. Shock, plain and simple. He's making the best of a very trying situation. Many of us have stepped forward to lend our expertise, and President Zimmer continues to be open to discussion in an extremely bipartisan manner. So, I will ask you one last time, Congressman, why should I sit and let you disparage *our* president?"

Congressman Antonio McKnight placed his hands palm down on the conference table, a grin tugging at his cheek. "What if I told you that Zimmer planned the whole thing?"

CHAPTER 5

There was a knock at the door. Cal lay sprawled on the leather couch in his suite at The Lodge, reading a W.E.B. Griffin novel. His favorite stories about the Marine Corps. He wasn't expecting company, as evidenced by his attire: a pair of workout shorts and no shirt.

Rolling off the couch and onto his feet, Cal padded to the door and looked through the peep hole. It was Travis.

Cal opened the door. "Did you just get in?"

"Yeah, it wasn't fun, but we made it down through the weather."

"You look like shit."

"Thanks. You mind if I come in?"

Cal swept his hand toward the spacious living area.

"How was the trip? You didn't tell me you were going."

Travis shrugged, stripping his coat off and putting it on a leather lounger. "It was fine. Mind if I grab a night cap?"

Cal motioned to the well-stocked bar, slightly concerned by his cousin's uncharacteristic restraint. Of the two, Travis was the more outgoing. Always had been.

After pouring a drink, the SEAL kicked his shoes off and sat on the couch, careful to keep from spilling the full glass. Cal sat across from him in an armchair.

"You gonna tell me what's going on?"

Travis sipped his drink, thinking. "I got an offer from the President."

"What kind of an offer?"

Another sip and a pause. "He wants me to come work for him."

A bark of a laugh escaped Cal's mouth. "What? You're kidding."

Travis shook his head. "He needs help, Cal."

"Help doing what, getting the country deeper in debt?"

The dirty blond CEO rested the glass on his knee and stared at his younger cousin. "Come on, Cal, be serious."

"I am being serious, Trav. What on God's green Earth would he want *you* to do for him?"

"He's getting it from all sides, doesn't know who to trust. Frankly, he's pretty down right now. You should've heard what Marge said."

"What did she say?"

"She said he should take a look in the mirror and grow a pair."

Another laugh. "Maybe she's right." Cal clasped his hands behind his head, leaning back.

"He's our friend, Cal. You wouldn't leave me to be fed to the wolves, would you?"

"Of course not, but you're not the President. What *exactly* does he want you to do?"

"He wants me to be his Chief of Staff."

"What happened to the old Chief of Staff?"

"He's still there, but Brandon doesn't trust him. Said he treats him like a child."

"Well, he is the youngest president in history."

"Cut the crap, Cal. I need to talk to you about this."

The smile left Cal's face. Travis was right; Brandon Zimmer was a friend, even if he was the President. "Are you really thinking about doing it?"

"Marge doesn't think I should."

"Why not?"

"SSI for one, but she also thinks Zimmer's on his way out."

Cal sat up. "What do you mean?"

"She thinks he'll either burn out or get forced to go."

"But he was appointed fairly. Who would do something like that?"

"Take your pick. I'll bet there are a bunch of politicians who are pissed about Brandon being in office. After thinking about it on the way home, I think she's right. If I was in line to be president and some rookie cut in line…you know how ruthless those bastards are."

Cal knew. If it were up to him, every crooked politician would be burned at the stake. "And you want to jump in the middle of this with him?"

"I don't know if I have a choice."

They sat quietly, Travis taking bigger and bigger gulps from his cocktail. Cal thought it was noble of his cousin to even consider the President's request, but he was afraid of the repercussions. "Wait, why did Marge go with you? Why didn't you take me or Dunn?"

Travis shook the ice in the bottom of the empty glass. "The President invited her to come."

The hair on the back of Cal's neck stood on end. "And?"

"He wants her to come to D.C. and help with appointing new cabinet members when the time is right."

Cal's eyes went wide. "He can't fucking do that! That's two of our top leaders, goddammit!"

His cousin shrugged. "That's what Marge said. She's already called to tell the President no. She said she'd do what she could to help from here."

"Well that's a relief. What about you?"

"I think I'm gonna do it."

"Jeez, Trav. Have you thought about the company, *our* company? Who will run things while you're off saving the President?"

Travis held out his tumbler. "You will."

———

WASHINGTON, D.C.

Senator Milton Southgate hadn't left his office since concluding the meeting with Congressman McKnight. He'd cancelled dinner plans with a friend, citing the worsening weather. In reality, Sen. Southgate had too much to think about. Unmoving in his dimly lit cocoon, a Civil War era clock ticking on the corner of his desk, the veteran politician replayed McKnight's accusations over and over.

At first he'd scoffed at the idea, but as the evidence stacked up precariously in the air between the two bureaucrats, Southgate found himself coming to believe what the popular Florida congressman was saying. "I've looked into this myself, Senator. Trust me when I tell you that I would not have brought this to you unless I honestly believed it was true. I don't want our country hurt by yet another scandal."

While the cautious senator didn't believe McKnight's motives, of which he was still curious, the revelations had stirred something in Southgate. The statesman from Arizona believed in order. He thought the new distractions of technology and social media a fad. He'd never carried a personal cell phone and never would. More than anything, he believed in his party's place in the history of the United States of America. As a teenager he'd had books on great Democrats like FDR and JFK. He never developed the charisma of such men, but Southgate believed in his soul that the Democratic Party was the party of the future, anointed from heaven to lead the United States, and one day a world under one flag.

Senator Milton Southgate didn't want to be president, and never had. He preferred to work behind the scenes to safeguard the dream, to take care of the people. His social welfare programs had helped untold thousands, if not millions, to find a better life. He truly believed that.

He'd known since the moment he heard the last President's speech appointing Zimmer to his post that a solution would present itself to right the wrong. The idea lay hidden, never once uttered from Southgate's lips. Instead, he showered the new President with wisdom and insight. Now...now he had a way out, a way to replace a piece of the Capitol chessboard.

He sat in his darkened office until after the antique grandfather clock in the foyer clanged midnight. Now was not the time for sleep. Now was the time for action.

CHAPTER 6

Cal pushed himself through the snowdrift, his quads scream-ing in protest. The gale slapped him in the face, telling him to turn back. He ignored the pain and ran on toward the rising sun. Sleep had never come after the conversation with Travis, which had ended with Cal flat out refusing to take over as CEO.

"I'm too young. I've got a lot going on right now."

"You don't think I was too young when your dad died? Come on, Cal, this is your company. It's time to man up and do what you need to do."

The memory burned almost as much as the strain. Plumes of white breath trailed behind, mimicking his feel-ings. Cal had never thought of SSI as *his* company. Sure, it was his dad's company, and he was the sole heir, but the com-pany had grown larger than his father probably ever would have imagined. Neil Patel's division alone easily financed the extracurricular activities Cal and his teams planned daily, off the official record, of course, and there were millions to spare.

Cal knew he was smart. He'd always had the mind to lead, but his heart couldn't be shackled to a boardroom. He preferred to be where he was, with his men, taking the fight to the enemy. He'd left the Marine Corps, but the Marine still lived in him. *I'm a warrior, not a businessman.*

Travis was going to Washington and Cal would soon be strapped to a desk, making sales calls, schmoozing with potential clients and reading endless reams of financial reports. The thought made Cal want to gag. Or was it the harsh pace he was pushing, snow caking his feet and calves?

He finally stopped at a small rise overlooking the campus, breathing deeply. It was the company cemetery. Five headstones poked their ivory tops above the snow. Reverently, Cal cleared the white powder from each of the tombstones, reading the inscriptions, remembering the men, his men, who had died on the snow-covered mountain in Wyoming. The others had been buried near their respective families, his good friend Brian Ramirez among them.

The final stone took the most time, not because it was larger; in fact, it was the smallest of the bunch. To Cal it was sacred ground, a place where he'd made a promise not long ago to the beautiful girl who now lay six feet beneath that very spot. His Jessica.

"What should I do, Jess?"

Only the slight wind against his running jacket answered, ruffling his collar. He stood thinking, wondering, hoping the answer would come.

CHAPTER 7

"Did you get me my job back?" Santos Lockwood stood in front of Congressman McKnight's desk, his hands behind his back, perspiring despite the frigid temperature Tony always kept.

McKnight didn't look up from his phone where he was Tweeting a picture he'd taken of the snow on the way into work with the description *#snowday* attached.

"I'm working on it. How's your hand? It's too bad about that shark. Big motherfucker."

Lockwood tensed. "The doctor stitched it up and it's healing." It would take a while to get used to the loss of his pinky and ring finger. Santos winced as he unconsciously flexed his injured appendage. At least McKnight had the courtesy to do it to his non-writing hand.

"Good. I hope it doesn't come between you and the ladies."

Lockwood took the mocking, used to it after years of knowing McKnight. The rest of the trip in Mexico had been more of a lesson in threats than a political junket. Every time they'd been alone together, the congressman had made some remark about having his family killed or cutting off his balls. The next second he'd return to his affable self, wining and dining with the real estate developer who'd invited them down to his new resort.

"What do you need me to do until we know?" Santos Lockwood was ready to be away from his unofficial boss. The duplicity was exhausting to be around, not to mention downright dangerous.

McKnight was always careful about what he said in his own office, especially after the recent scandal involving the NSA's snooping. "Come over to my place tonight and we'll talk."

Lockwood nodded and went for the door. Already on thin ice, he was happy just to have something to offer his old friend. He could only imagine what would happen if his usefulness ran out. Lockwood shuddered at the thought, closing the door quietly behind him.

Senator Milton Southgate had been waiting for thirty-seven minutes. He counted down the seconds as he watched sheets of ice blow past the elegantly framed window. A beat before the thirty-eighth minute ticked in Southgate's head, Secretary of State Geoffrey Dryburgh burst into the room, his wavy red hair curled neatly behind his ears. Loud and boisterous by nature, Dryburgh was not what one would think of as a particularly good candidate for the diplomatic post. What the casual observer didn't know was that the trim figure with ruddy cheeks, whose family hailed from the hills of Scotland, and was rumored to be a descendant of William Wallace himself, was a certified genius. After graduating with three majors from Harvard, Dryburgh had gone on to become the youngest partner in the history of New York's prestigious Kleinman, Shauver and Bosch law firm, waging war against corporate America one win after another. But what had made him sort of a folk hero, a man of the people, was that he'd founded and run a popular micro-brewery, Dryburgh Draft, all while rising through the ranks of New York City's best attorneys.

Cunning and overwhelming in public engagement and election battles, Dryburgh was a natural politician. The self-appointed voice of the working man. His first run for pub-lic office had been a dare on a celebratory night thrown by a drunk partner in Dryburgh's law firm. He'd won in over-whelming fashion, now having worn a path through the New York State House, through the U.S. Senate and his current post. He had the pedigree Southgate needed to use. He also had the smell of the presidency, already being touted as a hopeful should Zimmer not seek re-election.

"Senator Southgate, I'm sorry I'm so late. I know how much you appreciate punctuality." Dryburgh always threw in a bit of a Scottish twinge when he was putting on a show. He liked to say that America was his home, but Scotland was his mother.

"I understand you're a very busy man, Mr. Secretary. Thank you for coming." Southgate hid his displeasure well, knowing that he needed Dryburgh's full attention.

"Come on, Senator, can't you call me Geoff? You're twice my senior at least!" The Secretary of State laughed at his own joke while the stoic Senator bit back the bile in his throat. He'd never liked Geoffrey Dryburgh, but he was open-minded enough to know that the younger generation enjoyed the show the Scot loved to put on.

"Only if you call me Milton."

"You've got a deal, Milton. Now, what was so urgent that we both had to come out in this God awful snow?"

"Why don't we have a seat and I'll fill you in?"

Secretary of State Geoffrey Dryburgh was an ambitious man. He'd fought his way up the ladder and meant to stay there. His first run for office had been a dare. Now politics was his life, the best game he'd ever played.

Never having spent any private time with the Senate Majority Leader, he'd been intrigued by the senator's invitation. Everyone in Washington knew Milton Southgate was a goodie-two-shoes, always worried about appearances and doing the right thing. This ran in sharp contrast to Dryburgh's public image. He was known as a high flying, some would even say flamboyant, pauper turned politician who wasn't afraid to get in shouting matches.

Dryburgh had money he'd earned by hard work and toil, and he wasn't afraid to flaunt it, much to the dismay of frugal stalwarts like Sen. Southgate. Privy to secrets most Americans would be shocked to hear, Geoffrey Dryburgh was a man in the know. He'd made it his business to be intimate with every detail of every case he'd ever taken on. He still knew the recipe and process for the wide variety of beers being made by his famous micro-brewery. That being said, nothing had prepared him for the story Senator Southgate methodically laid before him.

"And you're sure about this?"

Southgate nodded solemnly. "I'm afraid so. I have my own people looking into it."

"Why can't you tell me where the information came from? If they told you, they told someone else. I'd hate for this to get out."

"My source assured me that I am the only one who knows. Now, let's talk about how we can contain the situation."

———

Congressman Antonio McKnight scrolled through his phone, jumping from one social media app to another. He'd made it his business from day one in office to stay at the forefront of any technology that could bolster his image. The Republican Party was failing to capture young and minority voters, but McKnight was part of the new breed. Young, handsome, and into many of the things twenty-somethings were into, namely being online 24/7. Other than the former president, he had the most online followers of any U.S. politician.

He wasn't married, so his nights were filled with cocktail parties and discreet liaisons. Early on he'd learned to keep his private life private. Despite his near constant use of technology, McKnight was diligent about security. If the last four years had taught him anything, it was that you never knew who was watching or listening. More than one cocky politician had seen years of work wiped away by a hacked cell phone or laptop.

The phone on his desk chirped. McKnight tapped the speaker button without looking up. "What's up?" the congressman asked his secretary, a middle aged woman named Linda, who was a better gatekeeper than a six foot six Samoan.

"Sir, Senator Southgate is on the line for you."

"Patch him through."

"Yes, sir."

Seconds later the call connected. "Are you there, Senator?"

"Good morning, Antonio."

"Good morning."

"I called to tell you that the investigation is progressing on our end."

McKnight leaned back in his chair, smiling at the ceiling. "That's good to hear."

An extended moment of silence. "Congressman, as I told you before, I will take care of this personally and I would appreciate your...discretion until we have a better idea of what we're dealing with."

"Not a problem. The last thing I want is to get in the middle of your business. If you need anything, please let me know."

"I will."

The line went dead. McKnight knew the old man was by the book, but he was positively giddy that the senator had moved so quickly. He'd made a good decision taking it right to the top.

McKnight silently congratulated himself, diverting his attention back to his last post that had already been shared on the web by over 100 followers in less than five minutes.

CHAPTER 8

"Stevie, you want me to make you anything for breakfast?" came the call from the kitchen.

Former FBI special agent Steve Stricklin, sweat-soaked, struggled to finish his last pull-up. "Sausage and eggs!"

While Stricklin hated the fact that he still lived at home, he couldn't complain about his mother's cooking. The widow waited on her only son hand and foot.

He nimbly dropped from the doorjamb pull-up bar onto the eighties era burnt orange carpet, flexing his six pack in the mirror. A couple jabs and a sweeping hook later, Stricklin grabbed his olive drab T-shirt, one of the last remnants of his time in the Marine Corps, and wiped his face.

In the last two months he'd had plenty of time to work out. He estimated that he'd put on at least five pounds of muscle, cutting his body fat to an acceptable eight percent.

After getting kicked out of the FBI in December, quietly of course, Stricklin had at first taken his sorrows to the bottle, stewing in his misery on the lower level of his mother's modest brick split level home. That had lasted for close to a month. Then something clicked. Overnight Stricklin gave up alcohol and refocused.

He was a former FBI agent, experienced in internal affairs investigations. Lucky for Stricklin that the Bureau had turned into a model of political correctness and allowed him to leave quietly, even providing a decent recommendation letter. It helped that Stricklin had experience manipulating situations where he had to cover his own ass, a fact that his superiors took into account before his dismissal. No one wanted him as their enemy, or so he thought.

If only things had gone differently. One day he was in the middle of the biggest investigation of his life, and then, just like that, his uncle, a popular congressman from Louisiana, was shot right in front of him. He didn't remember much after that. He never knew whether the alcohol or the blow to the back of his head had more to do with that, but he woke up on the steps of the Hoover Building (FBI headquarters), a group of administrative assistants pointing and taking his picture. That was a bad day. His superiors linked him to the crime, with the help of certain unnamed witnesses, thus ending his FBI career.

Stricklin didn't blame himself. He never did. Once again he'd been the victim of events outside of his control. Sure, he'd conducted an investigation outside his official duties, but he thought his initiative would be awarded, not condemned. They'd even made him sign paperwork promising to never divulge the information he'd already uncovered.

Bullshit. That piece of paper had held his tongue for a month, but his ego wouldn't let it go. In his mind, there was one person responsible for his fall. One man who'd plagued his career in the Marine Corps and in the FBI. Every other idiot called the man a hero. He knew better. His nemesis was one of the "unnamed sources" that led to his disgrace. He knew that now. The same man torpedoed him as a platoon commander during his time in the Marines, making him look like an idiot in front of company and battalion commanders.

Stricklin walked over to his desk, eyes resting on the over-sized cork board, papers pinned neatly in groups. Smack dab in the middle was a picture of his nemesis, a man who had ruined his life, an enemy whose name made Stricklin's blood boil. It was so unfair, but the tide would turn soon. Revenge would be sweet. And the best part? Stricklin sneered. Cal Stokes didn't even know he was coming.

———

CAMP SPARTAN, ARRINGTON, TN

Daniel Briggs, a former Marine sniper, and Cal's right hand, adjusted the tie holding his blond ponytail. "What did you decide?"

Cal stared out the snow-encrusted window in his living room. "I don't know."

"When does Travis need to know?"

"He didn't say, but I'm sure he wants my answer soon."

The man who SSI operators called Snake Eyes stood up and walked to the window. "It's not all bad. Maybe it's time for a break. We've been running pretty hard."

Cal and Daniel had forged a deep friendship over the preceding year. Rarely apart, the two Marines had planned and conducted countless operations on American soil.

Sometimes they talked about it, how much their new profession was like a kid being given anything he wanted. They had the assets to do more than most federal agencies.

To the warriors, it was the best of both worlds: play with guns and take care of the good 'ol U.S. of A. While Cal was more brash in his approach, the always stoic Daniel, Bible ever in hand, kept the train from derailing. He was the buffer to Cal's rage, the calming influence.

Cal knew his weaknesses, his short temper, an inability to keep his mouth shut, and countless others. That was what bothered him about Travis's ultimatum. Not only was Cal the last person who wanted to run a large corporation, he was also introspective enough to know that his personality would not lend itself well to the daily grind of a CEO.

"I don't know what he's thinking. You couldn't pay me enough to work in D.C.," said Cal.

"Even if Brandon asked you?"

"He's knows better than to ask me. Seriously, the only thing worse than me running SSI would be working on Capitol Hill."

Daniel couldn't disagree. He probably knew Cal better than anyone. Cal's disdain for politicians could almost be compared to his hatred for terrorists and criminals.

"Could Dunn run the company?" Todd Dunn was SSI's head of internal security, and played a similar role for Travis Haden that Daniel did for Cal.

"No, I asked. Dunn's probably not the right fit anyway. He's too good at what he does."

Daniel felt for his friend. He knew Cal's sense of duty would probably win over. It was his company after all. "I don't see a way out, Cal."

Cal huffed, shoulders slumping. He didn't want to let his cousin down, let alone the employees of SSI, but…

Cal's head snapped up, eyes bright. "I have an idea. Come on."

Daniel turned in surprise, Cal already slipping his arms into the well-worn cold weather coat. "Where are we going?"

Cal grinned. "I think I found a way out."

Shaking his head at his boss's attitude swing, the sniper followed Cal out the door.

Cal opened the conference door without knocking. Travis, Marge Haines, Todd Dunn, Neil Patel and Dr. Higgins were in the middle of a heated debate. Travis looked up, annoyance clearly etched in his scowl. "Do you ever knock?"

"Sometimes. Hey, I know how we can both get what we want."

"What are you talking about? Are you trying to weasel your way out again?"

Cal ignored the jab. "Look, I know you think I'm the obvious choice to take over for you, but I don't think you've thought it through."

Travis raised his hand. "How many times do we have to talk about this, Cal? This is *your* company. We've got a lot of good people counting on us. Do you want to let them down?"

"Of course not. That's why I don't think I'm the right fit."

Closing his eyes, Travis dropped the paper he was holding onto the conference room table. "Okay, you've got my attention. What do you propose?"

Cal smiled. "I think Marge should be CEO."

CHAPTER 9

CAMP SPARTAN,
ARRINGTON, TENNESSEE
11:57 A.M., FEBRUARY 28TH

No one said a word after Cal's declaration, not even Marge "The Hammer" Haines. Cal looked around the room. "Can any of you give me a single reason that Marge can't take over?"

"It's not that easy, Cal," said Travis.

"Why not? She's way more qualified than me and she's already cleared for everything I am."

"She's still considering the President's invitation."

"No offense, Trav, but letting one of our leaders go is one thing. Two is fucking crazy."

"He does have a point, Travis," offered Dr. Higgins, finger tapping his chin slowly, considering.

Travis turned to Haines. "What do you think?"

Haines took a moment to respond. "It is an intriguing offer..."

"See, I knew it!" exclaimed Cal.

"...but I already have a lot on my plate. I'm not sure it's the best thing for the company. Do I need to remind you that I'm the only female employee at Stokes Security International? What will your teammates say?"

Cal laughed. "Are you kidding? They fucking love you. It's not like you're an outsider. You're one of us."

More than a few SSI operators had felt The Hammer's raw skills on SSI's training mats over the years. If that weren't enough, she'd started training with the teams on the gun ranges and in the live fire complex. She'd even earned a well-deserved thumbs-up from Gaucho after a particularly brutal training exercise. "That's one loca lady," he'd said, a huge compliment coming from the Mexican badass.

"Look, we need to look at this thing for what it is, a business. If we were a traditional corporation, would the board vote for a former Marine without even a college degree, or an attorney, skilled in the art of courtroom battle and used to rubbing elbows with businessmen and politicians?"

The room digested Cal's words. Travis finally looked up. "Well, Marge, what do you think?"

Haines shrugged, nonplussed. "If it's unanimous, I'll do it."

The vote was unanimous with not a dissenter in the group.

"Cal, you want to tell me what I should tell the President?" asked Travis.

Cal shrugged. "That's not my job. I'm not the boss." A grin was already plastered on his face.

Travis lifted his hand, extending his middle finger. "Okay. If we're gonna do this, you get to come visit the President with me."

"But…"

"That was not a request, Cuz. It's your idea, so you can help explain it to the president."

Cal was trapped. Instead of stepping in one hole, he'd fallen the other way, right into the viper's pit. "Fine, but you're paying for us to fly first class."

———

THE WHITE HOUSE

President Brandon Zimmer shook the Japanese Prime Minister's hand, bowing slightly. "I look forward to seeing you again."

The prime minister left without a word, followed by his entourage. Zimmer walked to the fire. "Who's next, Ellen?"

Ellen Hanson, the president's secretary, was another hold-over from the last president. She looked at the calendar in her hands. "You've got the next thirty minutes free for lunch, and then you have Secretary of State Dryburgh at two o'clock."

Zimmer held back a groan. He and Dryburgh were roughly the same age, but something about the boisterous Secretary of State always annoyed him. Either way, he was stuck with the man for the foreseeable future. "What's that meeting about?"

Ellen referenced the calendar. "Updates on Ukraine, Iraq and Syria."

"Is General McMillan joining us?" He'd come to value the chairman of the Joint Chiefs's input. The Marine general had a way of distilling intelligence and operations that was both practical and insightful. McMillan was an integral part of Zimmer's team.

"No, sir. I believe the general is in Afghanistan."

Another wrinkle. Since taking the oath of office, Zimmer had made sure there was always a neutral party in attendance when he met with the charismatic Secretary of State. Zimmer knew his head of international affairs had ambitions higher than his current post. He wasn't the only one in Washington who wanted to be president, but no one else was as close to the throne as Dryburgh.

President Zimmer was finishing the last bite of his club sandwich when Secretary of State Geoffrey Dryburgh stepped into the Oval Office.

"I'm sorry, Mr. President. Ellen said you were ready for me."

Zimmer wiped his mouth with a monogrammed napkin. "That's okay, Geoff. I just finished." He stood to greet his guest, somewhat perturbed by the fact that Dryburgh was tall enough to look down on him.

"I'm glad we finally get some time one-on-one, sir. Sometimes it's nice to have a meeting without all those nosey staffers." Dryburgh flashed his brilliant smile, shaking the President's hand.

"I've been meaning to have a sit down with you, but as you can imagine, it's been a bit of a zoo around here."

Dryburgh laughed. "I can only imagine, Mr. President." He threw in a wink for effect. "How about I give you a quick rundown and then we'll chat?"

Zimmer tried to hide his surprise. Maybe he could have a working relationship with the man after all.

Exactly twenty minutes later, Dryburgh had concisely outlined the hot topics for the day, and answered the President's
immediate concerns with precision. It seemed that they were
on the same page.

"I've gotta say, Geoff, I was a little concerned coming into
this."

"How so, sir?"

"To be honest, I thought you might be a bit less…asser-
tive on the international stage."

Instead of being offended, Dryburgh smiled. "I understand. You'll have to remember that I serve at your discretion.
Your predecessor, although a man of the people, could sometimes be…how to put it lightly…he could be a bit soft with
foreign leaders. To his credit, he expected the best of people.
As his Secretary of State, I was bound by his policy, not mine."

Zimmer listened intently, wanting to get a full grasp of a
possible new ally. "And now?"

Dryburgh went serious. "My family comes from a
country that was subjugated for centuries under the guise
of familial trust. In many ways, the United Kingdom still
controls Scotland. I am a student of history, Mr. President.
I know that for every well-meaning politician, there are five
more jockeying for power behind the scenes. I had a good
working relationship with your father, God rest his soul. He
was a Democrat, but an American patriot, just like me. He
knew the importance of a strong international stance. I had
assumed, rightly I hope, that you were the same."

"I'll admit, a couple years ago I was a little more naive
than I would have liked, but I've since come to have a better
grasp of the truth."

A smile returned to Dryburgh's slightly freckled features. "Then I'd say we're on the right path, Mr. President."

"I'm glad to hear that."

"I'm glad to say it, sir. Maybe if you really learn to trust me, one day you can tell me how it felt that day you fell into the presidency." This time Dryburgh's wink made Zimmer laugh.

CHAPTER 10

Senator Southgate sat tapping his index finger on his knee, mimicking the ticks of his great-grandfather's clock, one of the few pieces the family had saved when Union cavalry ransacked their pastoral home in southern Kentucky. He hadn't moved in almost an hour. It was what he did: carefully weigh the pros and cons, ins and outs of an important move.

He was slowly digesting the news he'd received from his contact in the Department of Homeland Security. It didn't look good. He hadn't found a smoking gun, but initial signs seemed to corroborate Congressman McKnight's accusations.

Southgate had to tread lightly. Although the ascendance of the new President had at first shocked Americans, Zimmer's poll numbers were climbing. His voting record, while short in comparison to the veterans in town, spoke of a new type of Democrat, a man who could reach across the political aisle. His handpicked team had done a masterful job at scheduling well-orchestrated events, further painting the young president into a modern day JFK.

Doubt crept in. The good of his party and the American people were at the heart of Southgate's concerns. He didn't have the slightest ambition to be president, but he did crave order. McKnight's revelations had the potential of destroying much of what Southgate had worked to build over the last quarter of his political career. It didn't help that he couldn't get the former president on the phone, or the fact that Zimmer seemed less decisive than Southgate would have thought. While he didn't have anything concrete, now might be a perfect time to capitalize on the President's weakness, even if the help came from a Republican congressman.

Meetings cancelled due to the record-breaking snowstorm, Southgate stared into the fire, ticking time, weighing his options and the fate of the new President.

<hr />

After a lingering kiss, McKnight rolled off of the naked intern with a grunt. "Why don't you get cleaned up."

The intern licked her lips beneath pouty eyes. "You sure you don't want to go again?"

"I've got work to do, honey. Maybe later, okay?"

The petite blonde took the hint and made her way to the bathroom while McKnight sat naked, checking his email. He was waiting for something, anything from Southgate. Not that he really needed the old man's help, but it would make his job easier. It would also keep McKnight out of the spotlight for the time being.

He didn't want the attention just yet.

A second later his phone registered a new message. Anyone tracking his account would think it was just another message from a fan, but it wasn't. Utilizing the coded script he'd devised, McKnight smiled. He'd soon have enough proof to incriminate the President and give the Democrats a whopping black eye. Then, in the middle of the mayhem, a new leader could rise; a man seeking to give tired Americans, who were overwhelmingly skeptical of the jobs politicians were doing in Washington, something different.

It wouldn't happen instantaneously, but McKnight was a patient man. Politics was a marathon, not a sprint. McKnight had his running shoes on and was ready to make his way to the front of the pack.

CHAPTER 11

The Secret Service escort waved them down as soon as they walked out of the jetway. Travis led the way.

"Good flight, Mr. Haden?" asked the smaller of the two agents.

"Please, call me Travis. We're in the same line of work, remember?"

The agent smiled. "Of course." He turned to Cal and Daniel. "Gentlemen, it's a pleasure to see you again."

Cal offered his hand. "How they hangin', Brett?"

Brett Stayer, a fifteen year veteran, and now head of the president's security detail, grinned. "Can't complain." He turned and shook Daniel's hand, offering only a nod. "We've got a Suburban waiting out front. Let's grab your bags and head out."

The three man team from SSI had at first declined the Secret Service escort. That was until Stayer had insisted, wanting to repay the debt his agency owed the two Marines from their role in uncovering (and keeping quiet about) the involvement of one of the former president's agents who'd plotted to kill the first lady.

After collecting their bags, the group stepped out into the cold.

President Zimmer looked up from *The Washington Times* and stood when the three men entered the presidential residence.

"It's great to see you guys." He shook everyone's hand.

"Will that be all, sir?" asked Stayer.

"Thanks for picking them up at the airport, Brett. Did we get identification for these guys?"

"Yes, sir. I'll have them waiting in the Oval Office."

"Great. See you in a few minutes."

Stayer left. The others took a seat around the dining room table. A butler appeared as if out of thin air. "Gentlemen, can I get you anything for breakfast?"

Zimmer spoke up first. "I'll have three eggs, over easy, with a sliced avocado on the side."

"Yes, Mr. President. And you gentlemen?"

Travis, Cal and Daniel put in their orders. The butler nodded without writing down a thing, an abrupt about face taking him back to the kitchen.

"He turned like a Marine," Cal observed.

Zimmer chuckled. "Good eye. Lester's fairly new around here. I'm his third boss. Before that, he retired from the Marine Corps as a Master Sergeant."

They made small talk, Travis explaining the transition going on at SSI.

"I won't say that I'm not disappointed about Miss Haines not helping me here, but I can see why you chose her to take over as CEO. Smart gal."

The butler returned pushing a cart laden with dome-covered plates. He served the president first, then Cal. "Thanks, Top."

Lester's eyebrow rose. "Marine?"

"Staff Sergeant Calvin Stokes, Master Sergeant. Sitting next to me is Sergeant Daniel Briggs. We won't talk about my cousin over there. He was just a SEAL."

The butler shook Cal's hand. "Master Sergeant Lester Miles, Mr. Stokes." He looked at the President. "I thought I told you to be careful about hanging out with Marines, Mr. President."

Zimmer laughed.

While serving the remaining guests, former MSgt Lester Miles explained that he'd been a machine gunner after graduating from Parris Island, only to be lat-moved to culinary services after someone found out that he'd grown up in a restaurant business, earning the title of head chef at the age of eighteen.

"You ever run into a Master Sergeant Trent?" Travis asked, knowing it was a long shot.

Miles looked up in surprise. "Master Sergeant Willy Trent?"

"Yeah."

"Willy was my NCOIC when they lat-moved me. Made the transition a lot easier. Good man. How do you gentlemen know him?"

"He's works with us," said Cal. "Keeps us fat and happy while kicking our asses in the gym."

Miles laughed. "That sounds like Willy. You tell him I said hello, okay?"

"Will do."

The butler nodded to the President and disappeared again.

Zimmer shook his head as he cut into his first egg. "Do all Marines know each other?"

It was Cal who answered. "Only the good ones, Mr. President."

After finishing their meal, the four men headed down to the Oval Office, shadowed discreetly by the President's security detail.

Stepping in after Zimmer, Cal immediately recognized the three men waiting.

"General McMillan, Secretary Dryburgh, Senator Southgate, I'd like to introduce you to my new Chief of Staff, Travis Haden, and his colleagues, my friends, Cal Stokes and Daniel Briggs."

General McMillan stepped forward first. "I know you're a SEAL, Mr. Haden, but I hope you don't mind if I give my fellow Marines here an oorah."

"No, sir. I'm used to it."

McMillan shook Cal's hand and then stepped in front of Daniel, who felt suddenly out of place. Almost reverently, the Senior Officer of the United States Armed Forces offered his hand to Daniel. When Daniel took it, the Chairman of the Joint Chiefs pulled Briggs closer, whispering something in his ear. Daniel nodded, looking slightly embarrassed.

"Do you two know each other, General?" asked Dryburgh.

"I know who Mr. Briggs is, Mr. Secretary." McMillan didn't explain further. Cal looked to his friend, eyebrow arched.

"Why don't we get down to business, gentlemen," suggested the President.

Everyone followed his lead, taking a seat in one of the lounge chairs. Cal kept his eyes on the President, all the while wondering why Senator Southgate seemed to be staring icy daggers at him. *What's got that old fart in a twist?* Cal figured it was probably the inclusion of Washington outsiders on the stalwart senator's home turf.

Cal couldn't have been more wrong.

CHAPTER 12

Senator Southgate spent most of the meeting nodding and observing the President's friends. They were outsiders, something Southgate didn't like. He had to be careful. They were the President's men, not to be taken lightly. He'd only just found out about the new Chief of Staff the day before when the request had come from the President to meet.

As he rode in the Lincoln Towncar back to his office, he replayed the exchange in his head, still not comfortable with the level of familiarity between the strangers and the President. It seemed as though Congressman McKnight's insights were accurate. But he needed proof.

The president loosened his tie. "I think that went fairly well."

Travis nodded thoughtfully. "No problem with McMillan, and I'd say Dryburgh was friendly enough. But Southgate…"

"It takes a bit to get used to him. My dad used to say that Old Southgate was the final wall holding the Senate back from bursting into the twenty-first century. He likes his order and rules with an iron fist."

"Do you think he'll be a problem?"

"I don't think so. He's by-the-book, but I think his heart's in the right place. A Democrat through and through."

Cal wasn't convinced. "I don't think he likes the idea of Travis being your Chief of Staff. Couldn't you feel the contempt coming off the guy?"

Travis shrugged, unaffected as usual. "I don't really care what he thinks. I'm here to do a job, for as long as the President wants me."

"Senator Southgate will be fine. If you have any problems with him, let me know," said the President.

Cal and Daniel left the Commander in Chief and his new right hand man to their business. They hadn't even been in town for half a day and already Cal was getting the itch to leave. "How about we go for a little walk?"

Daniel nodded, unfazed by the mountains of snow outside.

Once they'd left the White House behind, walking between the wall of shoveled snow on either side of the road, Cal asked. "What did General McMillan say to you?"

Daniel colored just noticeably. "He wanted to say thank you."

"You know him?"

"I knew who he was, but he obviously knows a lot more about me."

"What do you mean?"

"He said he knew about the CMH, and that he knew why I didn't get it."

The Congressional Medal of Honor is the nation's highly military award for valor in combat. Then Sgt. Briggs was nominated, and would have received the medal if he hadn't gone to the former president personally and asked for the nomination to be pulled. The president had done so, mostly because Daniel had been part of the team who'd saved the president's life.

"Is that all he said?" Cal knew all about the award.

"No. He said if I ever needed anything, not to hesitate to contact him."

Cal glanced at his friend. "Well, that could be helpful."

Daniel looked up for the first time. "What do you mean?"

Cal grinned mischievously. "It's always nice to have a Marine general on retainer."

———

Secretary of State Dryburgh told his driver to take the long way back to the office. He needed time to think, time to digest what he'd just witnessed. Southgate was obviously pissed, sitting there with a stick up his ass, seething no doubt.

Without being told, Dryburgh guessed that the three men he'd just met weren't just former military; they were very likely current operators either in one of the government's intelligence agencies, or possibly working for a private security corporation.

In his travels and in his time in government, Dryburgh had met his fair share of hired guns. While the president's friends didn't look like meatheads, they certainly had the subtle look of ruthless warriors.

The Secretary of State picked up his secure handset and pressed a preset number. "This is Secretary Dryburgh. I need you to pull a couple files for me."

———

They were back in sight of The White House after a chilly thirty minute jaunt when Cal's phone buzzed. It was Neil Patel, SSI's vice president of R&D and a virtual Rolodex with important contacts eclectically gathered over the years of mingling in the higher echelons of tech and moneyed society. "What's up, Neil?"

"You somewhere you can talk?"

"Yeah."

"Just thought you should know that we're already getting pings on your records, both through headquarters Marine Corps and the FBI."

The tech whiz had his automated systems, which he'd personally programmed, constantly on the lookout for information requests on key SSI personnel. He'd explained it to Cal by equating it to a Google Alert. "You know when you set a Google Alert for a certain term or keyword, and whenever something's posted online with that string of words, you get an alert?"

"Sure."

"Well, this kinda works the same way. If someone working at the CIA goes to pull up information on you, I get an alert detailing who did it and the information they accessed."

"Wouldn't you have to have access to the CIA's network?"

Patel had just shrugged, as if to say that such a thing were no big deal.

"Who put in the requests?"

"One came from the State Department, and another came from the FBI."

"That has to be Dryburgh and Southgate," Cal said.

"How do you know that?"

"We just had a meeting with them."

Neil whistled. "It sure didn't take them long. How did you piss them off?" Neil knew of Cal's dislike of politicians, a trait he'd had since their time together at the University of Virginia.

"I was very nice. Ask Daniel."

"He was very nice," said Daniel, loud enough for Neil to hear.

"You want me to look into it?" asked Neil.

"Let's hold off for now. I'll bet they just wanted to know who we are. I'd do the same thing."

"Okay, but let me know if you need my help."

"I will. Thanks, Neil."

Daniel looked at his friend once the call ended. "What are you thinking?"

"I think I better keep my mouth shut or I'm liable to piss off a whole bunch of people in this town."

CHAPTER 13

The pub was packed. Federal employees mingled with college co-eds over drink specials inspired by the crappy weather. With the blizzard wreaking havoc on local roadways, many employers opted to allow their employees to work from home or have a day off. The crowd at the old bar wasn't necessarily rowdy, but it was easy to see that many had spent most of their day in the tastefully appointed establishment.

Steve Stricklin seemed to be the only patron not enjoying himself. He sat in a corner booth, much to the annoyance of the proprietor, who had more than once asked to have the table for the swelling crowd.

Stricklin had finally said, "FBI," and flashed his old bureau ID card.

The bar manager had relented and left the ornery customer alone. It wasn't unusual to have federal employees flash their badges around, demanding special attention. It was all in a day's work for pub employees, but it didn't keep them from thinking of those badge flashers as arrogant pricks.

Stricklin sat nursing his club soda, counting down the seconds until leaving. His guest was over an hour late, and the former FBI agent's patience was paper thin. A moment later, there was a commotion at the door. Stricklin looked up. It was just a group of new girls in matching pink tank tops squealing after finding their friends. His gaze lingered a moment on one particular cute co-ed, a blonde with extremely large breasts.

"You like the blonde or the brunette?"

Stricklin jumped, spilling some of his soda in the process. He turned to his right. The man who'd made the comment stood an arm's distance away, a ball cap casting a shadow on his face. *How did he do that?* Stricklin thought, unnerved by the silent entrance. "Huh? Oh, neither."

The guest motioned for Stricklin to scoot over, taking his spot. "What are you drinking?"

"Club soda," Stricklin answered.

"Teetotaler?"

"No. Just wanted to keep a clear head."

A waitress had seen the new addition and stepped up to an order. The man in the ball cap looked up. One eyebrow rose as the waitress made eye contact. Congressman Antonio McKnight put a finger to his lips, motioning toward the rest of the bar. The waitress smiled, nodding. "What can I get for you, sir?"

"I'll have a scotch, neat."

"And your friend?"

"He'll have a cranberry juice."

McKnight winked at the girl, who left promptly to fill their order.

The Florida congressman turned to Stricklin. "We need to talk about the timeline."

Stricklin sat up straighter. "What? I thought you said—"

McKnight held up a hand. "The situation has changed."

Stricklin huffed. "I've been working on this for months, and now you want me to push it back. Maybe I should—"

McKnight cut Stricklin off with an icy glare. "I didn't say anything about pushing it back."

"But you said—"

"Do you ever shut up?"

Stricklin's mouth closed. He'd stepped over the line.

"That's better." A smile returned to the congressman's face. "Now, like I was saying, the timeline has changed. We need to speed things up."

Stricklin seemed mollified, and waited to see if he could ask a question. McKnight nodded. "Ask your question, Steve."

"Why the change?" Stricklin's tone mellowed, now taking on a subservient hint.

"It looks like they just made things a lot easier for us."

"Who? How?"

McKnight grinned. "I just found out your old pal Stokes got in town this morning, and he's been hanging out with the President."

A wide smile, the likes of which he hadn't had in months, spread on Stricklin's face. The pieces were fitting into place, the most important of them being enemy number one, Cal Stokes. If he could only take Stokes down with the President... well, that would be Karma finally on his side.

Travis Haden yawned into his hand. It had been a long day. First the early flight from Nashville, and then a full day of meetings. Travis knew he'd have to get used to it. Being the President's Chief of Staff was a twenty-four hour job. Nights and weekends included.

He'd met so many people that he couldn't imagine keeping everyone's name straight. Ellen, the President's secretary, said she'd have a handful of prospective aides in the next day for interviews. "You'll need someone to help you, Mr. Haden."

Travis didn't doubt it. At SSI he'd managed his daily tasks mostly on his own. At the White House, he could have a small army of staffers at his beck and call. *One step at a time*, he told himself.

There was a knock at the door.

"Come in."

The door creaked open. Cal stepped in the near barren office, save the quickly growing stack of files on the desk, followed by Daniel Briggs.

"What are you guys still doing here?" Travis asked, having assumed that his cousin would have caught the first plane back to Nashville, or at least to SSI's second headquarters in Charlottesville.

"The President's secretary called and said Brandon wanted to see me. I thought I'd stop by before going in."

"Something I should know about?"

"I thought you would know that's why I came here first."

"He didn't say anything to me," Travis said. "What time is the meeting?"

"Seven."

Travis looked at his watch. "You want me to come with you?"

"You don't have to. I see you've got enough to do." Cal pointed to the stack of paper on Travis's desk. "You still sure you want the job?"

Travis exhaled. "Yeah. It's no SEAL Team Six, but probably more stressful."

"We'll stop by on our way out."

President Zimmer was hunched over, working at the coffee table, his suit coat and tie laying on a side chair. He looked up when Cal and Daniel walked in, his eyes slightly sunken from the strain of the day. "Hey, guys. I was just gonna get a cup of coffee. Want anything?"

"This place got any beer?" Cal asked, followed by an elbow from Daniel.

Zimmer laughed. "That sounds better than coffee. Do me favor, press the button that says butler on my phone and tell them what we want."

Cal picked up the phone sitting on the side table and put in their order. Not two minutes later, Lester Miles walked in balancing two Sweetwater 420s and a bottle of water. "I should've known you were the one ordering the beer," Lester offered with a grin.

"What can I say, Top? You can take the Marine out of the Corps, but you can't take the Corps out of the Marine."

The butler handed out the perfectly chilled beverages and excused himself. President Zimmer was the first to take a healthy swig of his beer. "That's good. I didn't know we had it."

Cal swallowed, savoring the hoppy taste. "It's a brewery down in Atlanta. We get it all the time in Nashville."

Daniel sipped his water, remaining silent as usual.

"Why don't you two have a seat. I had something I wanted to ask you," said Zimmer.

Cal noted the hesitation in his friend's tone, and took his seat slowly. "What's up?"

Zimmer motioned to the mess on the coffee table. "Just playing a little catch-up, or, a lot of catch-up." He sat back into the sofa cushion, taking another swig of his beer. "What did you guys think of our meeting earlier?"

Cal and Daniel looked at each other. "We were just talking to Trav about it," said Cal. "General McMillan's a good guy, use him."

"I have. He's a lot like you two. No bullshit." The two Marines nodded. "What about Dryburgh and Southgate?"

Cal took a moment to respond. "Why don't you let Daniel answer that question? I'm trying to be more PC while I'm here."

"Daniel?"

"It's like me and Cal talked about, Southgate is suspicious. We're not sure it was the best idea introducing us."

"Why not?"

Daniel looked to Cal, who nodded for him to continue. "Having Travis as your Chief of Staff is one thing. Inviting your friends, who happen to be in the line of work that we are, to meet two very senior politicians could make you look bad."

"I don't know if they'd look at it that way. Besides, they don't even know what you guys do."

Cal interrupted. "They will soon. We've already gotten word that right after our powwow two inquiries went out requesting information on me, Travis and Daniel."

"And you know this how?"

Cal shrugged. "Neil. There's not much the guy can't do with a computer."

President Zimmer sat quietly, digesting the information. On the one hand, he'd expected Southgate and Dryburgh to be suspicious. He would have been too if the roles were reversed. On the other hand, he was the President of the United States. Something about having others go behind his back, however necessary, sent early warning signals flashing in his mind.

Zimmer was no novice to the political game. He'd been around it since birth. The problem was, unlike before, when he'd fought tooth and nail for his seat in Congress, and built a team from the ground up, he was now in someone else's position. It was like switching wives on a whim and being expected to be the same husband the other guy was. Impossible.

Cal felt for the young president. He knew it had come as a complete shock to Zimmer when his predecessor had handed off the keys to the kingdom. Hell, the whole world had seen Zimmer's reaction on live television.

But Cal knew Zimmer was made of tougher stuff than others might think. He wasn't just a pretty boy wanting to be famous. Since meeting the former congressman from Massachusetts, and truthfully not liking him at first, Cal had seen Zimmer grow in his views of the world and in his passion to affect change. He knew his flaws and wasn't afraid to work hard. In short, Cal trusted the man with his life, and for the blunt Marine who trusted few, that was a very big thing.

"Look, we'll be fine. We know how to watch our backs. It's you I'm worried about. You look like someone just pissed in your beer."

The comment snapped Zimmer out of his trance, his face registering surprise. "What?"

"I said, you need to buck up, Mr. President. They don't call you the leader of the free world for nothing. I know the whole thing sucks, and you didn't have a clue this would happen when you agreed to step in as vice president, but that's all done. There's no going back. You've got a job to do."

President Brandon Zimmer looked at his friend for a long time and then nodded.

CHAPTER 14

The rest of the conversation had gone well, Cal promising to help in any way he could, from the safe confines of SSI, of course, and the President's attitude improved.

"He seemed a little more down than I would've thought, Cal. You think something else is going on that we don't know about?"

Cal and Daniel made the final turn to Travis's office. "I don't know. I think he would have told us."

"It just seems strange. The Brandon we know is so *not* down in the mouth."

"Tell me about it. Maybe it's just the job. I wouldn't put that on any sane person, believe me."

THE RUSSIAN EMBASSY, WASHINGTON, D.C.

Secretary of State Geoffrey Dryburgh sipped his vodka out of the hand-carved mug that was no bigger than a standard shot glass.

"Tell me what's new in Mother Russia, Igor."

Igor Bukov, the Russian Ambassador to the United States, refilled his guest's glass with a vodka he'd said came from the most expensive distillery in his country. The two men had known each other for years, first meeting in the early nineties when Dryburgh had visited Russia on a business trip to seek out new sourcing partners for an American liquor distributor. Back then, Bukov had been CEO of one of Russia's largest vodka brands, Bukov Vodka, a company founded by his grandfather. The businessmen turned politicians had hit it off instantly.

"It's still very cold, my friend." Bukov spoke with only the minuscule hint of a Russian accent, a testament to his European education.

Dryburgh pointed to the window. "And you don't call this cold?"

"This feels like summer to me, Geoffrey." Bukov raised his glass in a toast, downing it again.

"What about the political climate? Any thoughts on our new president?"

Bukov shrugged, noncommittal. "Not my place to say."

"Come on. You're best friends with the leader of Russia. Don't give me that crap, Igor." The jab came with a friendly smile.

"I would not call what I have with my country's president a best friendship, more like a healthy working relationship."

Bukov was downplaying his role in the Russian government and Dryburgh knew it. The wily Russian, while never having served a day in the Russian government prior to his appointment as ambassador to the U.S., was a seasoned veteran of his nation's political process. Over more than a few shots of his family's stock, Bukov had once admitted to a not-quite-so-inebriated Geoffrey Dryburgh that his family had bankrolled numerous politicians over the years. He'd even bragged about having a hand in the current president's ascendance.

"Okay, then how might you *assume* your president feels about our new president?"

Another shrug, another shot of vodka. "I can only assume that our country's leaders are still trying to understand President Brandon Zimmer, much as I assume you are? He is still young in your political process, is he not?"

"He is, but he shows a lot of promise." Dryburgh decided to press his friend. "Tell me, was the decision to help Crimea cede from Ukraine a test to see what President Zimmer would do?"

"How could I know? I'm a lowly ambassador, my friend. Besides, to say that we helped that happen..."

Dryburgh laughed. "Don't give me that, Igor. You know goddam well what happened. I've read the reports. We know how you did it and exactly who helped."

"As I said, I have nothing to do with Russian policy. I merely serve at my president's pleasure. To turn the question back to you, shouldn't you be the one helping to shape your president's foreign policy? How did you tell him to handle the Crimea incident?"

To call it an 'incident' was laughable. Russia made a land grab, in front of the entire world, and got away with it.

"We were still working off the last president's policy at the time. I've told you since his departure that he was not what I would call my perfect partner in the international game."

"And yet, President Zimmer did nothing?"

This time it was Dryburgh who shrugged. "A minor hiccup. We're putting things in place as we speak."

Bukov's hooded eyes looked up. "Something you would like to share?"

Dryburgh ignored the question. "What about Kaliningrad?"

"What about it? Would you like a history lesson?"

"Kaliningrad, formerly Königsberg. Used to be the most militarized area in the Russian Federation. Once the headquarters of the Baltic Military District, now the home of Russia's Baltic Fleet and a Special Economic Zone."

"Did you memorize that for my benefit? Bravo, Geoffrey. Very good."

"No." Dryburgh took another sip from his drink. "I've recently had communications from my counterparts in Lithuania and Poland. They have concerns about your expansion in Kaliningrad."

"What type of expansion? Economic? Surely they can't be worried about that. As I understand, they've reaped the benefits of Kaliningrad's growth as a manufacturing hub."

"No, not economic. Military expansion."

"That's ridiculous. You remember what happened when it was rumored that Russia would house nuclear weapons in Kaliningrad? And that was a rumor!"

Rumor indeed. Dryburgh knew it to be true. The Russians had a way of believing their own half-truths.

"Why would the Russian Navy be excavating large portions of the coastline?"

"How would I know?"

"Not to mention the deployment of troops dressed as common tourists."

"Now that is preposterous, my friend. Do you also believe the rumors that our top scientists are trying to clone Lenin and Stalin in order to take over the world?"

"It could happen."

"Now you are teasing me, Geoffrey."

Dryburgh grinned. "Guilty."

Ambassador Igor Bukov shook his head. "So, why all the questions about a small strip of land in the Baltic Sea?"

Dryburgh weighed his options, knowing he had his friend's attention, the Russian a virtual funnel to his own president. He had to push Zimmer to the brink, make him uncomfortable, trip him up enough to make a disastrous decision. With the added support of Senator Southgate, and his criminal accusations, Dryburgh would be there to pick up the pieces, to grab the presidency in his capable hands and lead America to its rightful place on the international scene. He also wouldn't mind showing his cocky Scottish cousins, who still didn't give him the deference he thought he deserved, proof that despite his inferior upbringing, he could become the most powerful man in the world.

The Russians were just reckless enough to take the bait, to push Zimmer without much incentive. Dryburgh knew what they wanted and planned to help them get it. In his mind it was an acceptable cost of doing business with the resurgent former Soviet empire.

Finally, he spoke. "I'll tell you this because we're friends, Igor." Bukov leaned closer. "I'm not sure that if there were to be an incident, say in Kaliningrad, that Zimmer would be prepared to handle it. We're still dealing with the policy debacle of our last president."

Bukov sat back in his chair. "Then it is a very good thing that it will not happen."

"It is, Igor, it is." Dryburgh filled both their glasses and raised his in the air. "To Russia's future."

"And to America's," Bukov added. They each downed their drinks, quickly refilling.

Put that in your pipe and smoke it, thought Dryburgh.

CHAPTER 15

The weather had cleared, allowing Cal and Daniel to book a flight home. They'd just finished packing when Cal's phone rang.

"Stokes."

"I have Mr. Haden on the line for you, sir."

"Thanks."

The phone clicked. "Cal?"

"Good morning, Mr. Bigshot. Already have someone making calls for you?" Cal teased.

The typical Travis chuckle never came over the line. "Listen, I need you to come to the White House. Something's come up."

"Can you tell me now? We were about to take off for the airport."

"No. I need you here, now."

"Okay. We can be there in twenty to thirty minutes, depending on traffic."

"The sooner the better."

73

The line went dead and Cal looked up at Daniel. "Looks like we're heading back into the lion's den.

It took them closer to forty-five minutes to get to the White House. The streets had been cleared of snow, but it seemed that every government employee in town was heading to work.

A Secret Service agent was waiting for the pair at the main gate. The only thing he said was, "If you'll please follow me, gentlemen." They were escorted to Travis's office. "I'll tell Mr. Haden you're here." The agent left Cal and Daniel to wait.

"What do you think's going on?" asked Daniel.

"I don't know, but did you see the extra security?"

Daniel nodded. He'd noted the beefed up presence as soon as they'd stepped out of the taxi.

Travis stepped into the small office. He looked like he needed a shower. "Thanks for coming, guys. You know I wouldn't have asked if it wasn't important."

"What's going on?" asked Cal.

"Early this morning, Russia made a play for Lithuania, much like they did with Crimea."

"I don't get it. What's that have to do with us?"

"It doesn't, but the next part does. Senator Southgate called the President shortly after midnight and asked him point blank about his ongoing relationship with SSI."

"And what did Brandon say?"

"He told him that we'd all met through his predecessor and that we provided him with security a couple of times."

"I'll say again, I don't see what this has to do with us."

Travis exhaled. "Southgate says an anonymous source has informed him that SSI is involved in illegal operations on U.S. soil."

"What? Where the hell did he get that from?"

"I don't know, but the President is pissed."

"Trav, you know as well as I do that there isn't a shred of proof anyone can produce."

"It doesn't matter. Southgate doesn't like us, and he sure as hell doesn't want the President anywhere near us."

Cal held back his *I told you so*. "Is there a point to this? Because I think we can still get on a flight before noon."

"You're not getting on any planes today, Cal. Now will you shut up for one second so I can speak?"

Cal nodded.

"The worst part is that someone is accusing you and Daniel of being accomplices in Congressman Peter Quailen's murder."

"Who the hell said that?"

"Southgate didn't say. He's giving the President until the close of business to tell him everything."

"Or what?"

"Or he'll request a special investigation of the President."

"Can he do that?"

"It's been done for much less."

"So Brandon could get a black eye for knowing us. Is there something you're not telling me?"

Travis crossed his arms. "Southgate didn't come right out and say it, but Zimmer was pretty sure that the senator was alluding to impeachment."

CHAPTER 16

Steve Stricklin took his time getting ready, massaging his post-workout sore muscles with a mixture of baby oil and rub-in tanner. His mother had already picked up his suit from the dry cleaner's, along with a new tie. He'd told her he had a job interview. She couldn't have been happier, especially after the FBI had so mistreated her poor Stevie, or so she thought.

Just as Congressman McKnight promised, someone had been more than happy to listen to the highlights of his incredible story. The person was so eager, in fact, that he'd even invited Stricklin to brunch at the Congressional Country Club in Bethesda, Maryland.

Three months earlier, he couldn't have imagined rubbing elbows with some of the most powerful men in the country. Gone were the days of running down Internal Affairs investigations in crappy little towns across the southeast. Stricklin imagined what his life would be like in three more months. A cozy new job? Television interviews? Maybe even a book deal?

The thought made him smile as he took his time forming the perfect knot in his tie. It was an important day. It wouldn't do to look anything but sharp.

———◆———

THE WHITE HOUSE

The smell of coffee was strong, like a preparation for an all-nighter.

"No, Mr. President, I have not yet gotten a response from the Russians." Secretary of State Dryburgh flicked a piece of lint from his knee and then returned the president's gaze.

"Do I need to get on the phone with their president?"

"I think we should wait, sir."

"The longer we wait, the sooner the media will get a hold of this."

"They already have. My office is getting phone calls as we speak."

"Dammit. How did we not see this coming?"

"Our intelligence assets say the Russians learned their lesson with Ukraine and were able to keep the operation under wraps. Hell, the Lithuanian leadership found out about it after we did."

"What are my options, Geoff? And don't tell me to wait." Zimmer felt like things were unraveling fast. First the call from Southgate, and now the Russians were making a play for a bigger piece of the Baltic region.

"You'd have to ask the Secretary of Defense, but I'd say we could start moving some of our assets into the area, standard stuff."

"What about the European Union? What are they saying?"

"Nothing yet. I think they're waiting to see how bad it is."

"And how bad is it?"

"No deaths that we know of, but they have taken over control of Lithuania's ports on the Baltic Sea."

"Do we know where the troops and ships came from?"

"Yes, sir. They came from..." Dryburgh looked down at his notes. "...Kaliningrad."

The president's secretary poked her head in the door. "Sir, I have the Russian Ambassador on the phone."

Zimmer looked to Dryburgh, who nodded. "Patch him through please, Ellen."

The secretary closed the door as Dryburgh moved closer to the desk so he could listen in on the conversation. Zimmer took a sip of his coffee and waited. The light blinked red on his phone and he pushed the speaker button.

"This is President Zimmer."

———

"You two need to lay low until I tell you otherwise," said Travis.

"We can hang out at the house in Arlington," suggested Daniel.

"Good. Go now. I've gotta see if there's been any word from the Russians."

———

Russian Ambassador Igor Bukov hung up the phone with a sly grin. He'd informed the American president that Russian forces had indeed seized control of Lithuanian ports, but not for any of the reasons the Americans might have believed.

"Mr. President, I would like to apologize for not informing you earlier, but I only found out about this incident moments ago."

"And what exactly were you instructed to tell me, Ambassador?"

"Our military was conducting exercises off the coast of Kaliningrad when our intelligence service received a message from a high level official in the Lithuanian government who had concerns about certain cargo shipments, possibly weapons-grade core, being delivered to their ports in the next twenty-four hours."

"I've been told that the Lithuanian government had no knowledge of Russian troop movements until it was too late. Are you telling me that's not the case?"

"I can only relay what I've been told, Mr. President. The Lithuanian government requested our assistance to deal with the situation, and that is what we did."

Bukov leaned back in his chair, rehashing the conversation in his highly analytical mind. Dryburgh had been right; President Zimmer seemed to be following the same path as his predecessor. Despite what had happened in the Ukraine, the American President didn't seem to have the stomach to stand up to the Russians.

Igor Bukov picked up the phone and pressed a button. In Russian he said, "Bukov for the President."

President Zimmer relayed the particulars of the phone conversation to his new Chief of Staff. Travis listened intently, shaking his head more than once. "Did he say what was supposedly in the shipments?"

"Bukov mentioned nuclear components."

"From where?"

"He didn't say."

Travis turned to Dryburgh. "Mr. Secretary, have you heard from Lithuania? Did they really ask for Russia's help?"

"They're calling every ally they have. I can only assume we were at the top of the list."

"So it's complete bullshit."

Dryburgh nodded. "I'd say so. The problem is that until Lithuania unravels the secret of the mysterious official, our hands are tied."

Zimmer slammed a hand on his desk. "Dammit. We will not allow the Russians to rebuild the Soviet empire. Travis, have Ellen call everyone in. Nobody's going home until the Russians have pulled their troops out."

CHAPTER 17

Cal's phone vibrated on the kitchen table. He snatched it up. "Stokes."

"Hey, it's Neil."

"What did you find out?"

"We're still sifting through Southgate's phone records."

"Come on, man. This is kid's stuff to you."

"I know, I know, but a lot of calls come in and out of the senator's office. A vast majority of them are encrypted or at least masked. I'm not sure if we'll have an answer for you today."

"That's not good enough. The deadline is five o'clock. I need something before then."

"But—"

"Listen, Neil, if we don't find out who's feeding Southgate with this line of horseshit, we all may be facing conviction in federal court."

"Cal, I know you don't want to hear this, but the President was part of—"

"Don't say it. I know. That's not the point. The point is someone is trying to torpedo the President. I'm not gonna let that happen."

Neil sighed. "Okay. I'll see what I can do."

THE WHITE HOUSE

The mood in the Situation Room was tense if not downright hostile. Split right down the middle, the President's advisors couldn't come to a consensus. The Secretary of Defense, Secretary of State and Chairman of the Joint Chiefs all wanted the President to send in a carrier group along with a full Marine contingent.

Everyone else, including the president's national security advisor, Attorney General and the Secretaries of Treasury, Commerce and the Director of Homeland Security, preferred a more cautious approach. To make matters worse, all communications coming out of Lithuania had ceased. The entire country was under some sort of blackout.

"Mr. President, let's not make any rash decisions. Our markets are volatile as it is. Any hint of military incursion could send us tumbling back into a recession," said the balding Secretary of Commerce, the most vocal of the dissenters. Zimmer made a mental note to see what he could do about replacing the man. He'd been nothing but a whiner since he'd entered office, rarely with a solution to go along with his complaint.

"I understand," answered Zimmer, "but I will not stand by and let the Ukraine debacle happen again."

When Russia had effectively seized control of Crimea weeks before, Zimmer deferred to his war-weary cabinet members. He'd been slammed by numerous publications for his lack of action, and conservatives had howled to any reporter within reach.

The Secretary of Defense spoke up next. "Mr. President, the director of the Central Intelligence Agency is on his way over now. Might I suggest we wait and see what he's learned from his people in-country?"

"Fine. Let's adjourn until he gets here."

———————

BETHESDA, MARYLAND

Steve Stricklin could hardly contain himself as he walked back to his car. The meeting with Senator Southgate had gone better than expected. Not only had the senator taken notes during their conversation, he'd also promised to do everything he could to either see him reinstated at the Bureau or placed somewhere in one of the many companies Southgate had relationships with. The icing on the cake for Stricklin was when his host had suggested the possibility of having to testify in front of a senate investigative committee.

"I'll do whatever you need, Senator," he'd said, already imagining the clicking cameras and pretty reporters asking for interviews. He couldn't wait to tell his mother about how he would soon be a celebrity.

———————

Senator Milton Southgate sat in the Congressional Country Club lounge overlooking the famous golf course, now covered in snow. He hadn't known what to expect from the former FBI agent, but was pleasantly surprised. Put together, good looking, and a former Marine, Steve Stricklin could be the perfect vehicle for what Southgate was planning. He would have to thank Congressman McKnight for the introduction.

The stickier situation was that of the president. President Zimmer had stepped over the line. Calling in CIA assassins to kill a terrorist in a foreign country, while still repugnant to the senator, could be ignored. Associating with a company implicated in the murder of an American, and a congressman no less, was absolutely out of bounds. He wondered what other secrets the president was keeping.

No, he would not stand idle and let the upstart from Massachusetts ruin his party. Southgate already had his hands full from cleaning up the mess left by the last president. Democrats were scrambling to keep their constituents happy. What America needed now was a strong leader, someone with a mind and heart to bring the country further out of its most recent recession and into the new world order. Secretary of State Geoffrey Dryburgh, while not necessarily Southgate's first choice, was certainly in a position to capitalize on his personality and international relations experience. Dryburgh had been on the presidential campaign trail before, but this time would be different, even though it would mean taking certain actions that would be more than a bit distasteful for Senator Southgate, such as his ultimatum he'd given Zimmer the night before.

Southgate stood and squared his shoulders to the snowy vista. He would do everything in his power to see that the threat to the Democratic Party, and more importantly, to America, was dealt with swiftly and decisively.

CHAPTER 18

Cal hadn't stopped pacing for the last hour. Without word from Neil, the ticking seconds felt more like a hammer on his chest. In contrast, Daniel sat quietly, seemingly nonplussed by the situation.

"Why don't you have a seat, Cal? There's nothing we can do."

Cal looked at his friend, annoyance clearly etched in his scowl. "How can you just sit there?"

Daniel shrugged. "It's not that hard. You just bend your knees a bit and sit on your ass."

Cal stopped his pacing and regarded the sniper, a thin smile finally appearing. "Are you telling me that you're not worried about going to jail and possibly taking the President with us?"

"I've been on the edge of the law more times than I'd like to remember. All I can say is that as long as I've done the right...no, the honorable thing, everything has come out okay in the end."

Cal snorted. "I swear every day you become more and more like some monk sitting on a mountaintop giving wayward travelers sage advice."

In response, Daniel lifted his legs onto the couch, crossing them yoga-like, with his hands resting on his knees, palms facing up. "What wisdom would you like this day, young traveler?"

Cal shook his head and laughed. He couldn't remember the last time he'd seen Daniel crack a joke. The Marine sniper preferred to stay in the background, mouth closed, eyes and ears open. "You really are a piece of work, you know that?"

Daniel nodded solemnly. "Such wise words from so ornery a man."

The jab was answered by a middle finger. "Fuck you, Snake Eyes," Cal said with a grin.

The secure phone in the kitchen rang. Cal hurried to answer it. "Stokes."

"It's Neil."

"Yeah?"

"Southgate's phone records are still a no-go. I think I may have something else, though. It's not much—"

"Spit it out. We don't have time."

"Okay. I was able to get into Senator Southgate's scheduling system. He's had a couple meetings this morning. His secretary doesn't put names to everything so I'm not sure who he met. Nothing jumps out as far as location. I thought you might be able to help."

"Read them off to me."

Neil did. He was right. Nothing seemed out of the ordinary. Cal repeated them to Daniel, who was now standing next to him.

"Who was he meeting at the Country Club?" Daniel asked, after pressing the speaker button.

"It doesn't say."

"Was it just one meeting?"

"It says meeting and lunch."

Cal knew they were grasping at possibilities. "Let's look at it another way. Did the meeting origination have any kind of time stamp? Does it say when it was scheduled?"

"I hadn't even thought of that. Hold on. Okay, I'm going through them one by one. A week ago, a month ago, three days ago…"

Cal tapped his finger on the table impatiently. Daniel stood waiting. Neil kept reading aloud.

"The meeting at the Congressional Country Club was scheduled…last night!"

"I knew it!" Cal exclaimed. "Are you sure there's no way we can figure out who he met with?"

Neil took a minute to reply, going through his mental list of hacking opportunities. "I've got it. If I can get into the country club's CCTV surveillance system, then maybe we can see whoever was coming and going."

"This is all we've got, Neil. Call me back."

Cal felt reinvigorated. They finally had a lead. It wasn't much, but it was something. Hopefully Neil could use his magic to lead them farther down the trail. The minutes were still ticking down until the President's timeline. The Marine in Cal knew they could not fail in this task.

NATIONAL BURDEN

President Zimmer nodded his head as if he was listening, but everything his Secretary of the Interior was saying went right past the distracted leader. Zimmer could feel his blood pressure rising and sipped water to calm his nerves. Maybe he should finally give in and ask The White House physician for medication. He was young and healthy, but the stresses of the job had been exacerbated by Senator Southgate's accusation. Zimmer knew that he technically was associated with a company that conducted black operations on American soil, but he also believed that such actions were needed to defend the country from those threatening the United States. If only he could make Southgate see.

SSI SAFEHOUSE, ARLINGTON, VIRGINIA

Neil called back ten minutes later.

"Do you have your laptop?" he asked.

"Yeah, let me grab it." Cal snagged the computer from the kitchen counter and brought it over to the phone. "I've got it."

"I'm sending you an email with a link. Click on the link when you get it."

A moment later, the email appeared on Cal's screen and he clicked on the hyperlink. The highly secure internet browser Neil had developed, and was now being used by a select group of private corporations, opened in a new window. Cal and Daniel watched as a screenshot of Neil's computer popped up.

"Can you see my screen?" Neil asked.

"Yeah."

"Okay, it took me longer than expected, but I finally got into the country club's security system. I figured that instead of me trying to go through the feed myself, having you two look with me might be helpful."

"Couldn't you just use your facial recognition software?"

"I'll be running it congruently. I just figured that you might want to do something rather than just waiting. I'll run the playback at about double speed, starting with the thirty minutes before and then after Southgate's scheduled meeting."

Cal looked at his watch. They didn't have much time. "Play it."

Neil did, and the three SSI men settled in to watch.

CHAPTER 19

President Zimmer said goodbye to his last appointment of the day. Normally he would've been working until eight, but he'd had Ellen reschedule the rest of his meetings. Senator Southgate would be arriving in a little over an hour and Cal still hadn't called. Travis had disappeared, telling the President he'd be right back. That had been thirty minutes ago.

Zimmer's mind raced. He would not take Southgate's accusations lying down. Even if Cal and his team couldn't produce the source, he would go down fighting. If he'd learned anything from his father, it was that Zimmers never gave up, always holding out until the end.

The swooshing of the reinforced door made the President turn.

"I'm sorry it took me so long, Mr. President." Travis looked worried, a fact that did not help Zimmer's disposition.

"Find out anything?"

"No, sir."

"How about we order up a couple drinks. Might help to settle our nerves a bit."

"I hate to say it, but I think you're right. Scotch or bourbon?"

"Bourbon, please."

Travis nodded and went to call the butler. Zimmer took a seat by the fire, remembering the days when his family had spent winter vacations in Aspen. His father had never spared any expense, always procuring a monstrous house with a roaring fireplace. Young Brandon Zimmer had often fallen asleep gazing into the glowing embers, his father and mother looking on.

He wondered why the memory suddenly appeared, quickly realizing that despite his father's nefarious end, he would've paid a king's ransom to have his father's advice at the moment.

Travis sat down across from the President, wanting to say something, anything that would help soothe the distressed leader. But there was nothing to say. It looked like their secret was out. Cal's father, Col. Calvin Stokes, had instituted the mantra of *Corps Justice* years earlier. It was a secret code known only to a few outside the confines of Stokes Security International. Zimmer was one of the few.

The code read:

Corps Justice

*1. We will protect and defend the
Constitution of the United States.*
2. We will protect the weak and punish the wicked.
*3. When the laws of this nation hinder the
completion of these duties, our moral compass
will guide us to see the mission through.*

Now the code would be lost. Travis had always feared the day would come that an outsider would twist what the brave warriors of SSI had done. It was a noble cause, defending America against its invisible enemies. Americans took for granted the layer of security provided by the visible efforts of the brave men and women in the armed forces and in law enforcement.

Most people didn't know about the behind the scenes actions of CIA spies, black ops troops, and organizations like SSI. It wasn't something you ran to the papers with. Citizens wouldn't understand. The warriors who conducted silent war on battlefields at home and abroad didn't want publicity. They knew it was better to sneak up on the enemy in the dead of night, and slither out with the task complete. As long as the mission was accomplished and the country was made safer, that's all that mattered.

But others didn't see it that way. Travis bet Southgate was one of those men. He didn't know the senator personally, but he guessed that the senate veteran had been part of his fair share of efforts to curtail the missions of American intelligence and military forces. In the minds of men like Southgate, it was unconscionable to pay a murderer for information, or to threaten a man with his life in exchange for intelligence. Travis had been on countless operations where the outcome, typically the saving of countless American lives, would have been prevented had he and his troops not applied the necessary force and coercion to get the job done.

Now, Travis wasn't naive enough to think that there were not others who used codes like Stokes' *Corps Justice* as an excuse to hurt others, and that too many times such criminals did it for their own gain. That's why it was so important to Col. Stokes and Travis that the only leaders allowed to green-light such missions be of sound mind, with a high moral sense, selfless and honor-bound. Travis had spent his entire time at SSI weighing the pros and cons of working outside law. If there was any possibility that federal or local law enforcement could take care of the situation, the buck was passed to them.

Barring a sign from God, Travis bet that Southgate would most undoubtedly label SSI as a criminal enterprise, unworthy of praise or adulation, only fit for condemnation.

Cal and Daniel watched the figures speed past the country club video camera. Neil started with the main entrance, figuring it was their best shot at identifying Southgate's guest. It was still a long shot, but they were all hoping to recognize one of the many faces flashing across the computer screen.

They'd seen Senator Southgate dropped off, seeming slow in his gait despite the sped up feed. The recording wasn't as clear as Cal would've liked. Again, the seconds and minutes were ticking by. He'd had another text from Travis asking for an update. The Marine answered the same way he had the five times before: *No news yet.*

"Hold on," said Daniel suddenly.

Neil paused the playback. "What did you see?"

"I'm not sure. Go back a bit, to when that group of four went in."

The video reversed, Cal and Daniel moving closer to the screen. "Right there, the guy in the back with his face down."

Cal squinted. "Holy shit."

"Who is it?" asked Neil.

Cal's blood boiled. "It's Steve Stricklin."

CHAPTER 20

Senator Milton Southgate strolled in through the back entrance, escorted by a member of the White House security. He was early, but that was okay. Let the President sweat a bit when he found out he had arrived and was waiting.

As they walked along the vaunted corridors of the symbol of the most powerful country in the world, Southgate admired every detail, from the molding to the paintings, the carpets and the valences. In his mind, the home of the leader of the free world had seen better days. He had a duty to protect the office of the president and the country. The last thing he wanted was word of the president's actions to get out to the public. Hopefully Zimmer would take the noble path and resign. If he didn't, the leader of the senate was prepared to do what he must.

They'd finally caught a break. While Cal and Daniel hurried to the White House, Neil tracked down the infamous Steve Stricklin. Cal and Stricklin's relationship went back to their time in the Marine Corps. Stricklin had been then Sergeant Stokes's platoon commander. To say the former Second Lieutenant was an ineffective leader was a major understatement. Stricklin's career as an infantry officer quickly derailed as a result of his own ego and inability to lead Marines. The only thing he'd been good at was deflecting blame and taking credit from others.

The thought that Stricklin had once again stuck his nose in Cal's business made the Marine tremble with rage. Not months before, Stricklin, who turned out to be the nephew of the now departed crooked congressman from Louisiana, Peter Quailen, had tried to link Cal and SSI to terrorist bombings, merely to advance his own career. Cal had thought that Stricklin's dismissal from the FBI would've taught the man a lesson, but somehow the egotistical prick had weaseled his way back into Cal's life. It would be the last time.

Agent Brett Stayer was waiting for them. "You guys sure like to cut it close. Southgate's already here."

"Is he with the President?"

"No. We have him waiting down the hall."

"Good. I need at least five minutes with the President. Can you stall Southgate?"

"I'll take care of it," said Stayer.

Cal and Daniel entered the Oval Office in a rush. President Zimmer and Travis looked up from their conversation. "I don't know if you should be here, Cal," said Zimmer.

"You want me here, Mr. President. Wait until I tell you what we found."

Zimmer and Travis listened as Cal told them about Stricklin. The President shook his head. "I don't understand. Why would this Stricklin guy want to take me down? I don't even know him."

"If I had to guess, it's all about him. This guy's been an asshole since the minute I met him, and he's only gotten worse. I think I was the initial target. He hates me, thinks I ruined both his Marine Corps and FBI careers. You're just an added bonus. I'll bet he's having wet dreams about going down in history as the guy who torpedoed an American president."

President Zimmer shook his head sadly. "So it's all a game? This guy wants to get his fifteen minutes of fame?"

"I'd say so." Cal noticed that his cousin seemed lost in thought. "What are you thinking, Trav?"

"I'm still not sure if Southgate will care. Stricklin probably produced some kind of documentation, real or fake, linking the President to us. It's his word against ours, and from what I've heard about Southgate, he's not a big fan of the CIA or security companies like SSI. What did you say he calls them, Brandon?"

"Mercenary havens. I think he'd like to see every private security company put out of business."

The door opened and Brett Stayer stepped in. "Sir, I'm sorry to interrupt, but it's five after five and I think I've stalled the senator for as long as I can. He's getting antsy."

Zimmer looked to his friends. Travis nodded. "Bring him in."

Senator Southgate walked into the Oval Office, his eyes narrowing upon seeing Cal and Daniel. "What are *they* doing here?"

The president answered with a hint of anger in his tone. "*They* are my friends, Senator, and they're here to help me explain the truth you so desperately want to hear."

Southgate scoffed at the comment. "I know the truth. The only reason I'm here is—"

Zimmer stood up from his seat, his temper rising. "The only reason you're here is that I'm giving you the benefit of the doubt, Senator. Don't forget that I am still your Commander and Chief, and I will be afforded the respect of the office."

Looking momentarily stunned, Southgate searched for the correct words. He hadn't seen this coming, having pictured the encounter differently. It was supposed to be him calling the shots, not the president.

Finally he said, "I apologize, Mr. President. You're right. Despite the circumstances, there is no reason I cannot be cordial."

"Thank you, Senator. Now why don't we have a seat and talk through this unfortunate misunderstanding."

Southgate looked at the President incredulously, but kept his mouth shut and took a seat.

Once everyone was ready, President Zimmer asked Southgate to proceed.

The senator coughed and opened the file he'd carried in. "As I mentioned last night, certain evidence has been provided to me that indicates your knowledge and complicit involvement with Stokes Security International, a company led by the men seated in this room."

None of the SSI men moved, their eyes glued to the senator. Their collective gaze kept Southgate from looking at them directly. He went on to describe various instances, including the murder of Congressman Peter Quailen in front of his own home, where SSI operatives, including Calvin Stokes, Jr. and Daniel Briggs, were involved both directly and indirectly in illegal activities on American soil.

Southgate looked up from his file, meeting the gaze of his audience. Again, no one said a word, a fact that slightly unnerved the senator. *Why aren't they saying anything?* He would've thought the criminals would have put up some kind of fight, maybe even screamed in his face.

Another cough and he continued. He described the president's ongoing relationship with SSI and the obvious threat to the nation's highest office. "If you cannot see the position this puts you in, Mr. President, you are indeed more naive than I thought."

Zimmer stared at the cocky man, deciding whether it would be better to be subtle or more direct. He chose the latter. "Are you finished?"

"I believe that is sufficient information to lead you to the correct course of action."

"And what course of action would that be, Senator?"

Southgate thought it would have been obvious. "For you to resign, Mr. President."

Zimmer laughed, not a chuckle, but a guttural belly laugh that lasted for a full thirty seconds. The others looked on with smiles as Southgate's eyes went wide.

"May I ask what is so funny?"

"You know what, Milton, I'll tell you what's so damned funny. You. You are so damned funny."

"I beg your pardon." Southgate began to rise. "I don't have to sit here and—"

"Sit down, Senator," barked the president. Southgate hesitated. "I said, sit down."

Face red with a flush of embarrassment and indignation, Southgate sat down, hands gripping the arms of his chair as his pulse thrummed.

With a gleaming smile, the president continued. "As I was saying, I'll tell you why this is all so funny. I would have thought that a veteran senator, who's no doubt been part of numerous investigations and dealt with his fair share of anonymous informants, would be smarter than to believe the lies of an egomaniacal, disgraced former FBI agent like Steve Stricklin."

Southgate's face went gray. "How did you—"

"How did we know Stricklin was your informant? Well, I'm not gonna tell you that, Senator. I'll let you figure it out."

The senator's mind whirled. He'd been careful. Never once had he spoken to Stricklin on one of his lines. When he realized that somehow the men from Stokes Security International had figured it out, illegally no doubt, his composure returned.

"I have the word of a former FBI special agent, who also happens to be a former Marine officer, that these men, these criminals, not only had a hand in Quailen's death, but also assisted you in capturing the presidency."

The accusation cut through the air like a bolt of lightning. Southgate could tell by the looks on their faces that Zimmer and his accomplices hadn't seen that coming. No one had a thing to say this time, so Southgate continued. "I had hoped not to bring that last part up, but you left me no choice. Now, if we can move on and discuss how we will handle your resignation—"

Before he could finish, the office doors opened and Stayer took a step in.

"Sir, you have a visitor."

Senator Southgate whirled on the Secret Service agent. "Can't you see we're busy?" he hissed.

Stayer ignored him. "Sir," looking to the President, "may I bring in your visitor?"

Zimmer wasn't expecting anyone, but he trusted Stayer. "Sure, Brett."

Stayer nodded and turned.

"What is the meaning of this?" Southgate demanded, glaring at Zimmer. "This was supposed to be a closed meeting, and now—"

Everyone in the room rose as if on cue. Southgate turned to see who the visitor was. His eyes bulged when he recognized the tall figure wearing a pair of faded jeans and a heavy winter coat with a fur trim. He looked ten years older than Southgate remembered, having last seen the man months before. Slowly, Southgate rose, knees shaking slightly.

The former president of the United States, Zimmer's predecessor, smiled at the men gathered in his old office.

"I happened to be in town today and I got a call from Brett. He said I might want to stop by and clear up a little misunderstanding."

CHAPTER 21

No one had seen the former president since the day he'd left office on national television. He'd retreated to his home in Chicago, refusing all callers, supposedly focused on raising his two daughters, and occasionally visiting his wife, the former first lady, who now lay in a vegetative state in a Chicago long-term care facility.

They all shook the president's hand, all except for Southgate. He didn't know whether to stand or sit, stay or go. *What is he doing here?* Southgate thought, unease welling in the pit of his empty stomach. Just when his plan seemed to be coming together, another wrinkle had walked in the door.

After the president greeted the others by name, a fact that surprised Southgate immensely, Zimmer offered his old boss the seat facing the low burning fire. "Why don't you have a seat, Milton. You look a little shaky."

Southgate nodded and did as he was told. Nothing about the evening's encounter was going according to plan.

He couldn't remember the last time that had happened in his long and distinguished career. "Mr. President," he said, addressing his former colleague from the senate, "I don't mean to be rude, but we were in the midst of a rather heated discussion. I'm afraid—"

"Don't worry about offending me, Milt. You and I go back a ways."

Southgate's faced reddened at the man's cavalier attitude. "Sir, I must insist—"

It was Zimmer who cut in this time, his voice sharp. "I suggest you sit there and listen, Senator, before you say something you'll soon regret."

Southgate doubted that greatly, but kept his opinion to himself. He had all the proof he needed. A few minutes wouldn't make a difference.

"I know this isn't easy for you, Milt, but I think I can clear this whole thing up."

There was no response from Southgate, who waited patiently, mulling.

"First, let me address the charges you've leveled against President Zimmer regarding my recent…Let's call it a job change. I'll only say this once, so I hope you're listening. No one, not President Zimmer, not my staff, not even my family, knew that I was going to step down. If there's anyone to blame, it's me."

The President waited for Southgate, whose face did little to hide his confusion. Every shred of evidence he'd been provided, every angle he'd investigated, pointed to Zimmer being part of his predecessor's decision. The sliver of doubt in Southgate's mind morphed into something more, a reeling swath of uncertainty.

"I know it may be hard to believe," the former president continued, "especially in this town where everyone seems to know secrets before they happen, but it is true. Now, let's talk about the gentlemen from Stokes Security International. I don't know the full story concerning your claims, so why don't you give me the abbreviated version."

Southgate straightened in his chair, regaining a portion of his calm. The air in the room suddenly felt stifling. He resisted the urge to adjust his tie, which felt like it was choking him slowly. "I, uh." He looked down at the folder in his hands, opening it slowly. "As I've already told President Zimmer, the corporation known as Stokes Security International has, on more than one occasion, conducted illegal para-military operations in the United States." He went on to explain, albeit haltingly, the acts he'd outlined earlier to Zimmer.

Once he'd finished, Southgate looked up from his lap, expecting a horrified expression on the former president's face. It wasn't what he found. Instead, the man looked at him, eyes sad, head shaking with a wistful smile. "You've really stepped in it this time, haven't you, Milt?"

All color drained from the senator's face. A simmering log popped in the fireplace, throwing a spark against the metal grate. "You can't tell me that the evidence—"

"Who did you get this information from?"

It was Cal who answered. "Special Agent Steve Stricklin, Mr. President."

The president turned to Cal. "What? The guy we had kicked out of the Bureau? That Stricklin?"

"The same, Mr. President."

The former president whistled. "I'd love to know how you met that pitiful excuse for a human being, Milt."

Southgate's mouth moved, but no words came out.

"Never mind. I'm sure you'll take care of that little problem, as long as President Zimmer decides to let you keep your job. Here's the deal, Senator. The boys at SSI are the good guys. They saved my life on more than one occasion. They've done the same for countless Americans. As far as Congressman Pete Quailen, he was a crook, plain and simple. We have the proof. In fact, do you remember the little video that surfaced featuring Quailen snorting coke, doing hookers and making illegal deals with his buddy?"

Southgate nodded slowly. Everyone in Washington, and countless millions outside of the capital, had seen the video.

"That was my idea, Senator, and it was SSI who found the evidence. But they were not the ones who killed Quailen. Ironically, after SSI brought him in for questioning, it was someone on Quailen's own team who killed the congressman to keep him from talking, in this very building."

Southgate face somehow turned even paler.

"You see, SSI's only concern is the well-being of this country. I didn't know such patriots existed until my second term. If it were within my power, I would tell the entire world how special these men are. I would build a monument to memorialize their contributions. They fight evil every single day. They don't ask for awards. They don't ask for acclaim. They only do it so that we can do our jobs, so that our kids can live to see an America that we can be proud of. Now, if there's anything else you'd like me to address, you'd better do it now."

The leader of the senate, a veteran of innumerable congressional battles, who ruled with an iron fist, turned his gaze to President Zimmer. "Mr. President, I would like to formally submit my resignation from the United States Senate."

CHAPTER 22

The mood in the Oval Office felt almost festive as the former president mingled with the others. Daniel had thrown two more logs on the fire, which now flared a lively orange as if reflecting the changing atmosphere. Lester Miles brought an overflowing platter of hors d'oeuvres that the men ate hungrily.

Southgate had left immediately after President Zimmer refused the man's resignation, instead suggesting the shaken senator take the night to decide whether he wanted to work with or against the president's staff. "I'd rather have you with us, Senator."

He'd left with a nod after tossing the file in the fireplace.

"What do you think he'll do?" asked Cal.

"I think he'll come around," answered their surprise guest, who now looked more relaxed than any of them had ever seen, sipping Yuengling straight from the bottle. "Southgate's not stupid. He knows how bad he screwed up. But he's been around the block a few times. His influence alone is enough to keep him around, but that's your call, Mr. President."

Zimmer tipped his own beer in a silent toast. "At first, my gut told me to let him run, but you're right, I'd rather have him on my side. I don't think he'll pull a stunt like that again."

———

Congressman Antonio McKnight smiled when he looked down at his cell phone. He'd wondered how long it would take Southgate to call.

"McKn—"

"You set me up." Southgate's voice sounded weak and quivering to McKnight.

"I'm sorry, Senator?"

"Stricklin, SSI, it was all a lie." McKnight almost laughed at the desperation in the man's tone.

"Look, Senator, like I told you when we first met, this Stricklin guy came to me and I handed it off to you. He only told me about being with the FBI and that he needed to get the information into the right hands. I never guaranteed its authenticity."

The only noise coming from Southgate's end was the muted sounds of traffic. He waited before replying, more soothingly this time. "Maybe I can help if you tell me what happened."

A laugh from Southgate. "Oh, I think you've helped enough. This makes me wonder how much of the story came from Stricklin and how much you concocted. Maybe I should tell the president about who introduced me to that idiot Stricklin."

"It doesn't matter to me. I'll tell him the same thing I just told you. What would I have to gain?"

A calming breath later, Southgate answered, careful this time. "You're right, I'm sorry." He hated saying the words, but didn't want the Republican to think he had the upper hand. "I'll let you know what else we find out."

The call ended. McKnight smirked. Taking a sip of the Argentinian syrah from his crystal glass, swirling the expensive gift in his mouth, the politician looked around his modest, yet tastefully appointed town home. Maybe it was time for an upgrade.

———————

The snowcapped landscape drifted by, the driver doing his best to avoid the potholes that popped up overnight. Southgate didn't notice any of it. He'd been duped and felt like a fool. He'd made a mistake, overstepped his own need for structure and appearance by not being as thorough with Stricklin as he should have.

He couldn't point the finger at McKnight because the congressman was right, he didn't have any proof except for the introduction. Southgate filed away McKnight's words to digest later. Maybe the upstart was up to something, but at the moment Southgate didn't have a shred of confidence that he could initiate a proper investigation. His political capital account read ZERO. It would look to the president like he was trying to shift blame, something the proud senator never did.

Already recovering from multiple shocks, the seasoned politician knew what he had to do. He picked up the pay-as-you-go phone he'd had his driver purchase earlier in the day and dialed a number from memory.

———

Mrs. Stricklin answered the front door in her nightgown. *Who could be calling at this hour?*

She looked through the peep hole and saw three men, maybe more behind, all wearing suits and trench coats.

"May I help you?" she said through the door, not wanting to open it for just anyone.

"FBI, Mrs. Stricklin. We'd like to have a word with your son."

Mrs. Stricklin's ears perked up. Her Stevie had been so happy over the past week. Maybe he was getting his job back. She quickly opened the door and let the men in, each man flashing their ID badge as they entered.

"Stevie! You have visitors!" Mrs. Stricklin called, rushing to put on a pot of coffee.

Almost a minute later, Steve Stricklin stepped into the kitchen, freezing at the entryway. "What's—"

Three of the four agents lifted guns that Mrs. Stricklin hadn't even noticed them carrying at their sides.

"We're here to take you into custody, Stricklin."

Stricklin put his hands over his head, all color drained from his face. He started to sob, much as he'd done throughout his childhood and teenage years. Stevie, always so innocent and tender with her. Stevie, always so quick to take offense, especially with his classmates. He never had many friends, no sleepovers, a thought that flared in her mind like a warning sign she'd missed.

The agents handcuffed her son and moved to the exit.

"Stevie? What's going on?"

Stricklin ignored his mother, instead almost slipping on the piss running down his leg and onto the linoleum floor.

"Stevie?"

No one said a word. No one answered her. All thoughts of returning to the nightly news gone, Mrs. Stricklin stood at the open doorway, tears streaming down her face, landing silently on the frozen ground.

It took every ounce of restraint in his body for Secretary of State Geoffrey Dryburgh to keep from raising his voice. He squeezed his phone, staring at the off-white carpet now gripped by his bare feet. The sound of the television in the next room, his wife catching-up on the weekly shows they'd missed on their latest trip overseas, barely registering through the pounding in his head.

How the hell could Southgate have been wrong? He was never wrong! He'd taken the old bastard on his word, taken steps to secure his own footing. And now Southgate was saying that Zimmer was clean?

Dryburgh wanted to punch something. In his youth he might have torn the Carolina beach decorated sitting room to shreds. But that wasn't him anymore. He had changed, matured, like a fine wine, or better yet, an aged whiskey.

Everything had been planned in his head. He hadn't told Southgate about his role in the Lithuania incursion. That was something he planned on keeping to himself, and Bukov would never say a word. He knew better. And besides, it wasn't like Dryburgh had told Russia to do it. He'd only nudged them in the right direction.

He had to find another way. The presidency had been so close, within reach of his oversized hands that now clenched open and closed. He was sick of reporting to the ineffectual Zimmer. He, Geoffrey Dryburgh, former United States Senator and now Secretary of State, should be the man leading the country.

Not one to feel sorry for himself, always looking for the silver lining, or at least an angle to weasel a win out of defeat, Geoffrey Dryburgh stood slowly. As the face of American foreign policy, the Scot knew every hot spot in the world. He'd thought the Russians the perfect ploy, but he'd underestimated Zimmer's newfound resolve. *Maybe there's another way.* Just as the thought pierced his subconscious, another took its place, adding depth, layers building already, a plan. He had to hit Zimmer where it hurt, where he had no choice but to react the way Dryburgh wanted. The perfect entrapment.

Dryburgh's lips curled into a wry smile. He called into the master bedroom. "Honey, I'll be in the office. Don't wait up."

CHAPTER 23

Cal had been so ready to get out of D.C. that he'd ignored his frugal ways and chartered a private jet for himself and Daniel. The pair was enjoying a leisurely room service breakfast (another splurge) in Cal's permanent suite in The Lodge, neither saying a word as they crammed huge bites of pancake and sausage in their mouths, all the while admiring the blessedly sun-soaked fields of snow through the oversized windows of the VIP quarters.

"Have you talked to Marge yet?"

Cal shook his head. "I thought we could head over later today."

"I'll bet she's revolutionizing the place." Daniel had come to respect SSI's only female employee turned CEO from the first moment he'd met her. Sharp. Beautiful. Cunning. Honest. He'd only heard the rumors of her past courtroom exploits. It was said that her name still sent shivers down many a CEO's spine.

"I can't wait to tell Travis that we should've given her the job a long time ago."

"I'd wait on that if I were you. I think he's got his hands full for a while." Sometimes all Daniel could do was sit back and shake his head at the constant ribbing between the two cousins. The situation didn't matter; one of them was always hounding the other, in a cousinly way, of course.

"Whatever. He stepped in that shit sandwich himself." Cal pushed his licked-clean plate away, rubbing his toned stomach. "Besides, when did you become such a Travis Haden groupie?" He said it with a grin. Cal never let up. It was his style. Always the Marine.

Daniel let out a rare laugh. "You two really should seek counseling."

Cal laughed, getting a tiny glimpse of the sniper's sense of humor, something he usually kept hidden. Before he could throw a comment back at his friend, his phone chirped, indicating an incoming text. "It's Marge. She wants to see me."

"Speak of the devil. Do me a favor and try not to piss off The Hammer."

Grinning from ear-to-ear, Cal flipped Daniel a friendly middle finger. Always the Marine.

"How was your trip?" asked SSI's newly appointed CEO.

Cal looked around The Hammer's spotless office. Somehow every glass top, including her desk, was smudge-less. Two small file folders graced her working space, perfectly aligned to the edge. "It was okay. Trav fill you in?"

Haines nodded. "What are you doing now?"

"Lots of shitbags out there, Marge. Me and Daniel were going to spend the day scoping out our database to see what we could rustle up."

Haines looked up from her laptop. "I've got something for you."

Cal almost rolled his eyes, but remembered Daniel's warning. He liked The Hammer, but he didn't like being told what to do. Biting back a smartass remark, he asked, "What do you have?"

Haines waved him over, pointing to her computer screen. Cal stepped around the skinny glass desk, suddenly curious. There was a picture of a man, probably in his mid-fifties, posing for cameras at some black tie event. "Who's that?"

"Leo Martindale. He's an old friend. I did some work for him a couple years out of law school."

"Wait a minute, is this the billionaire?"

Haines nodded. "Leo's done well. His company, Dale and Moon, manages close to one trillion dollars in assets. Everything from stocks to real estate."

"I'm confused. What do you need me to do?"

"It's delicate. Leo called yesterday, confidentially, of course. He wanted me to fly up to New York City to talk to him."

"About what?"

"He wouldn't say, just that it was important."

"Marge, I don't mean to tell you how to do your job, but usually it works best if you tell people what you want them to do and then tell them why."

Haines frowned, until she noticed Cal trying to hold back a smile. Her shoulder bounced slightly with a silent chuckle. "You almost had me. Is this what you do to Travis?"

Cal shrugged, his face looking like a five-year-old sheepishly telling the truth. "I had to at least try."

SSI's new CEO shook her head, smiling this time. "Like I was saying, he wouldn't tell me what it was about, but it was important enough that he wanted to send his jet to pick me up."

"And you need me to...?"

"I want you to fly up there."

"No way, Marge. I just got home. I've got a lot to do."

Haines exhaled, reminding herself that Cal was actually the boss, seeing as he was the sole owner and all. "I know Leo. He wouldn't have asked if it wasn't important. I told him that I just took over here, and he suggested I send someone of equal stature, someone who could keep their mouth shut, and help if possible. Travis is with the President. That leaves you."

Hopping on a plane to visit a spoiled billionaire was the last thing Cal wanted to do. He could feel his killer instinct going rusty, his trigger finger most of all. "What about Dunn or Neil? They're better at that kind of stuff than I am."

Haines didn't budge. "No. It has to be you. You can't tell me an all-expense paid trip to New York City wouldn't be nice. Besides, he could end up being a client."

"Have you looked outside, Marge? You think it's bad here? They've got snow six feet deep up there."

Crossing her arms, eyes not leaving the stubborn Marine, Haines waited, tapping her index finger like a professor waiting for a student to vocalize the only answer available.

Cal huffed. "Fine, but on one condition."

"Name it."

Cal snapped his fingers, a thought coming. "Two conditions."

Haines made a "give it to me" gesture with her right hand.

"First, I take anyone I want with me."

"Okay. And your second request?"

Cal cupped his chin, rubbing his two-day stubble. "This guy pisses me off, I leave."

"Done."

CHAPTER 24

The faint scent of lemon, or was it orange, probably the remnants of the White House cleaning staff's furniture polish, lingered in the air of the President's private sitting room, a part of the residence. Senator Milton Southgate waited patiently, hands crossed on his lap. The President's butler had delivered a decaf earl grey tea moments after he'd arrived, setting it on the hand-carved oak coffee table in front of the visitor. Southgate hadn't touched it, worried that he might spill it with his trembling hands.

He'd had the night to think about his next steps, still wondering whether the President might simply ask for him to step down. It was not outside the realm of possibility. Stranger things had happened during his time in the senate, including a pair of senators, male and female, who'd been caught by an intern, fondling each other in a deserted hallway. Southgate had taken swift action against the two independently married senators, each of whom should've known better. It wasn't that the senate leader was a prude, but to do such a thing in the hallowed halls of congress, well, it was unacceptable.

If he were president, there was no doubt what he would've done had he been in Zimmer's shoes. That was what had made him reconsider his initial declaration. The President hadn't told the Secret Service to detain him and hadn't accepted Southgate's resignation.

Maybe he'd misjudged the young president. He'd, of course, known Zimmer's father, more of a conservative Democrat than Southgate, but still a good man, a worthy political ally. The information from Stricklin and McKnight had tainted his hopes for the new president. He could admit that he'd been wrong, painfully so. It had happened a handful of times over the years, but never to this degree. He'd let his elitist confidence cloud his judgment. Humbled, Southgate stood when President Zimmer entered, alone this time, looking every bit the youthful leader that JFK had been.

"Good afternoon, Mr. President."

Zimmer strolled over, smiling, not a hint of condescension in his demeanor. "Senator Southgate, I'm glad you called."

"Thank you for making time for me, sir."

President Zimmer motioned to the couches where the two men sat down, Zimmer almost lounging while Southgate sat ramrod straight.

"Please tell me you've reconsidered your offer from last night, Senator."

"Yes, sir. I have."

"That's very good to hear."

The President could tell that Southgate wanted to say something, their recent confrontation obviously holding the man's tongue. "I'd really like it if we could start over, Senator. I think it's a major understatement to say that we got off on the wrong foot."

Southgate nodded, uncomfortable in his present position. He was on unfamiliar ground, always used to having the upper hand. "Yes, sir. I would appreciate that. I cannot begin to apologize for the way I acted. If there was any way—"

Zimmer raised his hand, as if to say any past mistakes should be forgotten. "Senator, would it be okay if we spoke man-to-man for a bit?"

Another tentative nod from Southgate.

"Good. Now, the way I see it, we need to work together. I've always admired the way you run the Senate. A firm hand. What I would like you to understand is that although I may be new, I am not inexperienced. You knew my father. I want you to know who I am."

Southgate tried to smile, but it came across as more of a grimace. "I'd like that, sir."

Zimmer nodded. "We may not always see eye-to-eye on everything, but that's okay. When was the last time anyone in Washington agreed on anything? The point is we need to have a strong working relationship, you representing the old guard and me the new generation of political leadership. Is this making sense to you, Senator?"

"I…I think so, Mr. President."

"Good, because I wouldn't want any more misunderstandings about where my intentions lay." Zimmer threw a wink at the old senator for good measure. This was not an ass-kissing session. It was a strategic alliance born out of a need to bind two recent enemies to a common cause. "Did you ever think about running for president, Senator?"

Southgate sat back slightly, suddenly befuddled, wondering if Zimmer was asking him an innocent question or framing an accusation. "I've been very happy with my position in the Senate, Mr. President. Besides, I'm not sure I have the best face for television."

He's right about that, thought Zimmer. *He looks more like an ornery headmaster.*

Zimmer chuckled, more at his thoughts than Southgate's attempt at humor. "Assuming we work together…how would you propose we do that?"

The question caught Southgate off-guard. He'd assumed the president would make his demands and send him on his way. "Well…I…I can assist you in any way you would like, Mr. President."

"Like how, specifically?"

Southgate squirmed in his seat, the room feeling smaller, the fire hotter by the second. "I could help you shore up any…how should I put it…lack of support within the party."

"That would be helpful. I'm not sure everyone thinks I'm the best man for the job." Another wink from Zimmer, another short exhale from Southgate. "What else?"

Southgate felt like he was coming unglued from the inside out. As an only child he'd withstood hours of grilling from his mother and father, one a teacher, another a preacher. All for the sake of his 'education.' Some days it was questions on history, other days it was rote retelling of passages from the Bible. Young Milton resented the after school studies, and the lashings even more. Once he'd had a taste of political power, where he held the might to pass judgment on others, he'd slammed the door on the uncomfortable memory from his youth. Sitting across from the president, the same feeling he'd felt as a child boiled to the surface.

"Mr. President, maybe if you tell me how I might be of assistance, I can do everything in my power to help." His eyes pleaded. Zimmer relented, almost feeling sorry for the old man. Almost.

"I'll be honest, I'm not sure about most of the staff around here, and I get the feeling that a handful of my cabinet members resent the fact that I'm their new boss. How about you help me figure out which ones to keep and which ones to replace? I'm sure you'd have a lot of ideas that would help."

The idea perked Southgate's interest. It was something he could do, despite his heavy workload. "Yes, Mr. President. That's definitely something I could help you with."

Zimmer clapped his hands. "Good!" Then his brow furrowed. "Are you sure you'll be able to fit it in? I mean, with everything you already…"

"Yes, sir. I'll make the time."

Zimmer sat for a moment, wondering if Southgate could see what was coming. The only feeling he got from his guest was that he either wanted to piss his pants or run away as fast as his legs could take him. Zimmer snapped his fingers, sitting straight up. "I've got it!"

"What's that, Mr. President?"

"I know how we can make this happen."

"But, I thought…"

"Senator, I'm going to ask you a very big favor, something that I've been trying to figure out for the past few months."

It felt to Southgate like the president was playing tug-a-war with his brain. "Sir?"

"I think I know how to not only repair our relationship, but to make sure we capitalize on our alliance. Senator, I'd like for you to be my new vice president."

CHAPTER 25

"He did what?" Cal blurted, grabbing the car door for support. He, Daniel and MSgt Trent had just arrived at the Nashville Airport to meet Leo Martindale's jet. Wind swept through the nearly empty parking garage, a testament to the recent weather and the endless list of cancelled flights. One lone traveler walked past them, braced against the wind, face covered with his hand, pulling a carry-on suitcase.

Cal pressed his ear to the phone, trying to shield it from the powerful gusts so he could hear Travis. "Did you say he made Southgate his vice president?"

"I know it sounds crazy, but I really think it's brilliant."

"Cuz, I don't know what you're smokin', but that might be the dumbest—"

"Hear me out, Cal. It would've been stupid to cast Southgate aside. For all we know he could've been an innocent participant in what he did."

"He told Brandon to resign! How the hell was that innocent?"

"Will you just shut up and listen. Jeez. Now look, I'm not a fan of the guy either, but we're running with the whole 'keep your friends close and your enemies closer' scenario. This way we can keep an eye on the guy. If he'd have gone back to the Senate, he would've been back on his home turf. The vice president is as powerful as the president allows him to be."

Cal hadn't thought about it that way. His snap judgment had been to can the guy, maybe even have him thrown in some high level federal prison. But then again, that's why he did what he did and never wanted to be in politics, a game where you were surrounded by your enemies every single day. "I'm not saying you're right, but maybe, just maybe, it's a smart thing to keep him under your thumb."

He could barely hear Travis's chuckle on the other end, another snow-laced gust stinging his face. "Don't worry, we'll keep him busy. What about you? What's this I hear about you going to New York?"

"Marge can't go, so she asked me."

"That doesn't sound like you. If I ever asked, you would've given me the finger."

"What can I say, cuz? She's just a better boss than you."

"Fuck you, Cal," Travis answered with a laugh. "Have a good trip. I'll call with any new developments."

"Cool. Watch your six, Trav."

———

EN-ROUTE TO PARIS, FRANCE

The customized Boeing 737 was Secretary of State Dryburgh's usual mode of travel when going overseas. Outfitted to his standards, high polish yet low-key, the seats rearranged at his own expense to look more like the small groupings of collaborative pods one might see in a tech company's headquarters, Dryburgh sat hunched over a table talking to a man roughly ten years younger, and a full head shorter with a mop of thinning hair. The man sipped his champagne thoughtfully, mulling over Dryburgh's offer.

"I thought you just wanted me along for the ride, Geoff. You know, to see Paris and all."

Dryburgh laughed at his friend's disarming way of downplaying his importance. Jonas Layton had been a billionaire since the age of thirty. He'd been one of the cocky young guns to take Silicon Valley by storm. They'd met five years earlier when Layton swept into New York to buy Dryburgh's booming brewery business. It hadn't panned out, with Dryburgh wisely holding on to his asset that was now worth almost double what it had been at the time, but the two had struck up a casual friendship. What started as a mutual admiration based on business savvy, soon turned into a bond built over trips to Vail, sails to Bermuda and jaunts to Southern Italy.

Both men had come from nothing, and now ruled their hard-earned empires with pride.

"Do you really think that's possible?" asked Layton.

"I'm not sure. That's why I'm asking you."

Layton closed his eyes, running a finger along his lower lip. "Do you know what that would do to the markets?"

"In the short term, yes."

"I don't understand. Why are you looking at this?"

Dryburgh shrugged, taking a pull from his always stocked stash of Dryburgh Beer. "I won't always be secretary of state."

Layton leaned forward, quickly glancing over his shoulder at the staffers across the row. "Is there something you're not telling me?"

Another shrug and another swig from Dryburgh. "I'm not sure if Zimmer will make it."

"And why would you say that? I hear his approval ratings are going up every week. Hell, I think I even like the guy."

"I'm not saying I don't like him…but there are others who don't think he should be sitting in the Oval Office."

Jonas Layton sat back against the white leather, staring at his friend. He wasn't stupid. With an IQ somewhere over 200, how could he be? There was something Dryburgh wasn't telling him. It was like getting a nibble of the carrot and not getting to see who was holding it. "Then why are you telling me? Shouldn't you be telling the president?"

"He knows. Hell, it was a shitty position to be thrown into. The poor guy probably wants to quit!"

"Now you're fucking with me."

Dryburgh smiled. "Sure. What politician in their right mind wouldn't hang on to the presidency for dear life? I know I would."

Layton tipped his glass toward Dryburgh. "So why the first question? What does it have to do with me?"

"I just thought that with your connections in the financial markets…"

"Geoff, I only dabble, I don't—"

"Don't give me that, Jonas. You probably understand it better than the guy that invented the market. Weren't you the man who developed the software that predicted what consumers would do based on a given advertisement?"

"Sure, but—"

"And aren't you the guy who's picked every congressional and presidential election correctly for the last four years, just for fun?"

"But—"

"Come on, Jonas. If there's anyone that can predict public sentiment, it's you."

Layton nodded. Of course he was the best. He didn't go around bragging about it, but Dryburgh was right, Jonas Layton was the master of predictions, so much so that many in the tech world had taken to calling him "The Fortuneteller." *Time* magazine had even done a recent article on Layton's second rising, from businessman to prognosticator. Companies were clamoring for his insight, often paying millions for him to run his analysis, knowing that the fee was a small price to pay in order to avoid failure.

He'd slowly made his way into the government, helped in no small way by Geoffrey Dryburgh, who'd introduced him to key contractors around the globe. He was a handy tool for politicians judging the landscape for an upcoming election or a parliament looking to craft the perfect piece of legislation the public could embrace. Then there were the highly classified consultations with intelligence agencies that were increasingly using artificial intelligence, much of it being developed by Layton's company, to automate the tracking of terrorists and criminals. If someone wanted a crystal ball, Jonas Layton was the closest they'd get to holding one in their hands.

The trip to Paris included three such introductions to European conglomerates looking to have just five minutes with the famous American. Layton didn't like being in anyone's debt, but considered Dryburgh to be one of the few exceptions. They were close, and as far as he knew, the politician was more than clean; he was sterling. An anomaly in the political game.

"I still don't understand why you need me for this. You know what'll happen if what you say will happen actually does."

Dryburgh downed the rest of his beer and set it on the side table, grabbing another from the ice bucket near the window. "Imagine what we *could* do if we *did* make it happen."

CHAPTER 26

The Gulfstream lurched to a halt, throwing the three companions forward in their seats. A moment later the co-pilot walked back into the wood-paneled cabin. "Sorry about that landing, gentlemen. Some idiot thought it would be funny to taxi before the tower gave them permission. We wanted to let you know that we do actually know how to fly."

The crew had been more than accommodating, each taking the time to walk back to the cabin and introduce themselves. It turned out that the lead pilot was a former Navy helicopter pilot, and he'd been delighted to have Marines onboard.

"Don't worry about it. Us Marines have been through our share of shitty take-offs and landings," said Cal, unstrapping himself from the oversized leather seat.

The co-pilot chuckled. "I'll bet you have. Oh, almost forgot, Mr. Martindale's assistant said there will be a car waiting for you at the terminal. They'll take you to the hotel."

Trent stood, stretching his huge frame, having to slouch to keep from hitting his head on the ceiling. "You mind if I ask where we're staying?"

"Mr. Martindale puts all his VIP guests at The Peninsula."

"Never heard of it."

The co-pilot grinned. "Trust me, you'll like it."

Cal was still admiring the inside of the black armored Bentley that picked them up from the airport when they pulled up to the gold tassel-encrusted awnings framing the entrance to The Peninsula New York. Inside the Bentley it smelled like fresh hundred dollar bills, along with a hint of buffed cow hide. It was also probably one of the only cars in the world that MSgt Trent could fit in comfortably. "I wouldn't get used to riding back here, Top."

Trent had his hands clasped behind his head, a contented smile displaying his mood. "Maybe I should ask for one of these during our next contract negotiation."

Cal laughed. SSI was frugal by nature, opting for high tech weaponry over exorbitant luxury. It was a throwback to his father's days in the Corps; Spartan, yet the tip of the spear. That wasn't to say SSI employees weren't paid well. They were. Compensation was above the industry average, and a healthy housing/living allowance was given to employees who opted to not live on one of the two company campuses.

"If you can convince The Hammer to buy you one, I'll drive you around, Master Sergeant of Marines," said Cal.

Trent's eyes popped open, a child-like excitement glinting playfully, adding to the ear-to-ear grin. "You're on, Mr. Stokes."

An Asian valet, dressed in a white high-collared uniform along with a matching pillbox cap, went to grab their bags, but each man insisted on carrying their own. Regardless, Cal tipped the man handsomely, having learned early on the importance of taking care of those who were caring for you.

"Thank you, sir. If there's anything you need during your stay, feel free to ask for Lin." The valet tucked the large bill in his pocket smoothly, bowing in the process.

"Thanks," said Cal, leading the way into the opulent entryway.

After a seamless check-in, they were escorted to their room, The Peninsula Suite. Normally a 3,300 square foot two-bedroom penthouse, graced with Murano glass chandeliers, the suite had been converted at the last minute to include one extra king-sized bed in the space usually reserved for the dining room.

"As per Mr. Martindale's request," said the bell-hop who'd given them a quick tour of the rooms, which included not only a colorful splash of tasteful art-deco inspired decor, but also a grand piano in the corner of the living room. Muted rugs covered marble floors, reflections cast up as they walked. A fully stocked kitchen invited perusal with the clear glass front refrigerator neatly arranged with colorful vessels and food stuffs. There were huge crystal vases bursting with fresh cut flowers in each room, mounds of tropical fruit held in silver bowls on tables and two enormous metal bins filled with ice and overflowing with expensive bottled beer and liters of Tennessee whiskey.

The three Marines tried to appear nonplussed, but the sheer elegance of the suite was overwhelming to men who were more experienced in the art of rolling up a shirt for a pillow and using a poncho-cover as a blanket.

"Will there be anything else, sir?" asked their guide.

"No thanks." Cal ran his hand along the window sill, admiring the view of downtown New York City, red and white lights streaming far below.

Daniel handed the man a tip and escorted him out, locking the door once he'd left. "What do we do now?"

"Martindale should be calling soon."

As if on command, the room phone rang. Cal answered it. "Stokes."

"Mr. Stokes, this is Leo Martindale."

"Hello."

"I hope your flight was okay?"

"It was. Thanks."

"Good. I know we weren't supposed to meet until tomorrow, but I'm right down the road. Would it be okay if I stopped by?"

Cal almost said, "You're the one paying for this, dude," but held his tongue. Instead he said, "Sure. You don't mind if we order some food while we wait?"

"How about I do one better? Let me bring dinner."

"Sounds good."

Cal replaced the receiver and looked up at his friends. "Wash your hands and wipe your asses boys, we're about to be served by a billionaire."

Leo Martindale arrived twenty minutes later, handling two large plastic bags laden with pizza boxes wrapped in brown paper. "I hope you guys are hungry," Martindale said with a smile that seemed more genuine than Cal would have thought. *Maybe this guy isn't a schmuck*, thought Cal.

It turned out that the gregarious billionaire had stopped to get four different kinds of pizza from four different restaurants. "I figured three Marines would rather eat some authentic New York pizza than some foo foo shit from Swankytown."

The three SSI men looked up, Cal almost choking on the huge bite of pizza in his mouth. Martindale laughed at the bewilderment on their faces. "Semper Fi, boys. Staff Sergeant Leo Martindale at your service."

It turned out that Leo had done a six-year stint in the early '80s in intelligence. As they ate the greasy oversized slices of mouthwatering pie, Martindale told them about how he'd left the Corps, gone back to school to get his degree, and then worked his way up the slippery Wall Street slope. He regaled them with stories from his early days as a stock broker, going from cold-calling, to networking, to landing his first big deals. In a community full of greed, where one broker would gladly backstab another if it meant a chance at a commission, Martindale had earned a reputation as one of the good guys. An honest broker. An anomaly.

"I won't lie. The crash of '87 almost bankrupted me. Luckily, I had a handful of clients that stuck with me. All but one still have."

"So when did you open your own place?" Cal asked, picking a hockey-puck-sized piece of pepperoni off one of the pizzas and folding it into his mouth.

"1990. I'd learned my lesson in '87. While I liked my broker, I thought there were things the company was doing that were a bit too risky for my taste. Funny thing is, well, maybe not so funny, but they invested heavily in the first tech bubble after 2000 and ended up closing shop. They should've been more careful, but by then they were getting desperate for returns. That guy ended up killing himself."

There was silence for a moment while they each digested Martindale's words and the last of their meals. Trent said, "I've gotta say, Leo, it makes us all proud to see a down and dirty Staff Sergeant make it to the top. Hell, Cal told us you were gonna be some corn-cob-up-the-ass kinda guy."

"Fuck you, Top," Cal said, slightly embarrassed, but still smiling. "It's true. Marge should have told me."

Leo was smiling too. A Marine never misses the chance to fuck with a fellow Marine, especially one that he likes. "I told Marge not to say anything. Figured it would be better if I handled that part. She said you weren't jumping up and down to come up here."

Cal shrugged. "I'm just a dumb grunt, Leo. Never been one for rubbing elbows with wealthy Wall Street types."

"Just know that I'm not one of those, what did you call them, Top?"

"Corn-cob-up-the-ass kinda guy."

"Right. I'm not one of those. I may have a lot of money, but I don't think I'm the only one in the room with that problem."

Cal adjusted himself in his chair. He wasn't comfortable talking about his money. In his mind, he hadn't earned it, his father had. Not a day went by that he wouldn't give up all his millions for more time with his mother and father.

"I can see by the look on your face that you don't like to talk about your checkbook," Leo continued, not swayed by Cal's frown. "But I don't believe for a second that you're just a dumb grunt. Five bucks says your two brothers here would say different."

Daniel and Trent nodded.

Cal threw his hands in the air. "Okay, okay. Let's stop talking about me. Leo, tell us why you wanted us to come."

Martindale's smile disappeared, his face serious. It reminded Cal of the look on his platoon sergeant's face the first time he'd gone out on patrol. "I think someone's planning on collapsing the U.S. stock market."

CHAPTER 27

The room was quiet except for the muted sounds of traffic from the street below, honks and the occasional screech. It was like Martindale had laid a grenade with no pin in the middle of the oriental carpet under their feet. No one wanted to touch it.

"What do you mean someone's trying to collapse the stock market?" Cal asked. "How is that even possible?"

Martindale threw his crumpled napkin into one of the empty pizza boxes. "I'm not sure it is, but I'm pretty sure someone's trying to see if they can do it."

Trent leaned forward, his shifting weight making the couch squeak. "I'm not a stock broker like you, Leo. I mean, I have a few bonds and whatnot, but I seem to remember certain safeguards being in place that wouldn't allow that to happen."

"Let me see if I can explain it in a way you'll understand." Martindale paused to gather his thoughts. The other waited patiently. "Okay, what happens after someone, say, loses a toe? Do they go on walking like before, or do they compensate with the rest of their foot?"

"They compensate," said Trent.

"Right. So that's kind of what I've noticed. Certain stocks have taken inexplicable dives. I've had my people do the research. These are reputable stocks. Nothing anywhere gives any indication of why their stocks went down."

"But isn't the market like the lottery? Crazy stuff we don't even know can affect it, right?"

"Yes, but to a point. Typically, if, as you said, crazy stuff happens, it doesn't affect just that one stock. Large scale ups and downs are just that, large scale. They affect many stocks."

Cal wasn't sure he understood where Martindale was going. "So you're saying someone is manipulating these stocks?"

"I can't prove it, but I think so. It's not unheard of. In fact, a book recently came out talking about something us veterans have known for a long time. Have you ever heard of high-frequency trading?"

All three men shook their heads.

"In a nutshell, there are companies that use highly sophisticated computer systems to move in and out of stock positions in a fraction of a second. They're capitalizing on minute changes that can drastically affect a stock's price by the time a traditional trading firm puts in their order," explained Martindale.

"So you're saying that between the time my day-trading account order is placed and when the purchase is actually made, these other guys are in and out selling for what could be a small increase, but I'm the one who ends up paying more?" asked Cal.

Martindale nodded, impressed. "Dumb grunt my ass. High-frequency trading's been around long enough that it's not a secret, at least to insiders. This new thing doesn't feel like that. This is more like someone's rigging the system."

"Have you told anyone?" Cal asked, still not sure why the billionaire had called SSI. Maybe Marge was a super stock whiz kid on the side.

"No, you three are the first."

"And you called us because…?"

"I knew I could trust Marge. It helps that the company was founded by a Marine who knew how to keep secrets."

"Wait, did you know my dad?"

Martindale nodded. "I did. He did some work for me in the late nineties. Helped with a few security analyses for companies I was looking to buy. Good man. I'd like to think we were friends."

Cal's father had never mentioned Leo Martindale, but then again, in those days Cal was wrapping up high school in Tennessee and heading off to college. He wasn't part of SSI other than the occasional take your son to work day. "That still doesn't answer the question. Why didn't you take this to the authorities, the SEC or the FBI?"

Martindale looked uncomfortable, not like he was trying to hide anything, more like he was trying to decide how honest to be with Cal. "Look, I know those guys are around for a reason, but the second I raise even a discreet flag, they'll be all over me. I'd rather not have the attention, if you know what I mean."

Something wasn't making sense. SSI didn't specialize in this kind of thing. Sure, they had Neil Patel, who could hack into anything and build technology that only Stephen

Hawking could fathom, but they were still a company full of warriors, doing what former military contractors did.

"Leo, I appreciate you telling us all this, but I'm just not sure how we can help. We're not really built for this sort of thing. I'm sure I can ask around and find a company that specializes—"

Martindale cut him off with an emphatic shake of his head. "No, it has to be you guys. I need people I can trust, a company with brains and muscle."

Cal stared at the man, trying to read his expression. "What are you not saying? Is there something else?"

Martindale's body seemed to deflate like a balloon, his shoulders slumping, the confidence gone and replaced by a look Cal had seen too many times. "I thought I could take care of it, or at least that my head of security could, but, well, I've gotten a couple threats."

"From whom?"

"I don't know. It was somebody who found out that I'd been looking into these stock dips. They said if I didn't back off they'd kill my family."

"What about your security guy? What did he do about it?"

"He started looking into the threats a week ago..." Martindale's voice trailed off as he stared at the coffee table stacked with pizza boxes.

Cal moved closer, placing a hand on Martindale's shoulder. "What happened, Leo?"

Martindale shook his head, pain etched into his face as he looked up. "I found him hanging from a noose in my garage yesterday morning."

CHAPTER 28

Secretary of State Geoffrey Dryburgh almost spit his orange juice all over the news summary one of his staffers had just delivered. He couldn't believe it. He read the headline again: *Senate Majority Leader Senator Milton Southgate appointed Vice President by President Brandon Zimmer.*

What was that crafty old man up to? Had this been part of his plan all along?

Dryburgh resisted the urge to crumple the five page report, instead grabbing a half-eaten croissant and flinging it across the posh hotel suite, narrowly missing the mirrored chest of drawers.

He used me.

The thought played in his mind over and over, only serving to incense the jet-lagged secretary of state even more. He had a meeting with the French prime minister in fifteen minutes or he would've gotten on the phone that second to wake up Southgate and give him a piece of his mind.

"Vice president. You sure as shit won't be for long."

Jonas Layton took his time getting ready. He'd already been to the workout room for a jog and a couple rounds on the elliptical. Feeling re-energized despite the six-hour time difference, Layton logged into his company's secure server and scanned his emails. A master of productivity, the wunderkind deleted, forwarded or replied to an assortment of close to one hundred messages in just under ten-minutes.

His morning routine complete, Layton settled in for his daily commute, a two-hour jaunt through the veins of the internet. The public didn't yet know about the new American vice president, but Layton found out quickly thanks to a high-level insider he kept on retainer. It was good to have informants who knew their way around governments, both foreign and domestic. It wasn't that he particularly cared about Zimmer's choice for his number two, but it did seem odd.

No matter. In a split second he'd moved on, carefully sifting through stock reports, doing his homework before his next meeting with Dryburgh. He would have the answer ready, but not in the way he'd thought.

By the time Dryburgh's meeting with the portly French prime minister finished, he'd had enough time to consider the Southgate situation. Where at first he'd taken offense, thinking that the senator had gone behind his back, he now believed he could use the situation to his benefit.

Sitting in a quiet corner of the hotel's preferred club, watched discreetly by his security detail, Dryburgh mulled his options, wondering how far he should go.

His greatest fear had been that Zimmer would ask *him* to be vice president. Yes, it was closer to the Oval Office, but only by geography. No, he would stay his hand, play along with Southgate's intrigue and bide his time. In Dryburgh's, and most other politicians's minds, there was much more prestige associated with being the American secretary of state than being the vice president. You had very little power as the supposed second-in-command unless the president willingly gave you more as a matter of policy. Dryburgh didn't believe for a second that Zimmer would have given him free reign.

As the master of foreign policy, however, Dryburgh could pretty much come and go as he pleased. So long as he didn't deviate too far from the President's agenda, he owned his fiefdom.

At least this way he wouldn't have the straight-laced Southgate on his tail. He'd be too busy doing the President's grunt work.

Dryburgh smiled at the thought, putting the pieces together in his mind like knights on a chessboard. That was him, a knight. Not a rook or a bishop and never a pawn. A knight moved erratically, never in a straight line, always unpredictable in the hands of a master player. Yes, that would be his strategy. Bob and weave. Shift and slide. He'd done it to his competition in business, easily outmaneuvering the lumbering behemoths, and he could do the same now.

The image of the white knight solidified in his brain as he sipped his herbal tea patiently, letting the tendrils of steam run up his face. How had he been so perturbed earlier? Now, the possibilities were endless. The only problem was deciding which weapon to use.

————◆————

THE WHITE HOUSE
3:30 A.M., MARCH 7TH

The clacking of his keyboard was the only sound in the heavily cubicled office, except for the hot air coming out of the overhead vent in regular intervals. Santos Lockwood sat glued to the screen, a stack of Styrofoam cups on his desk, crumbs of his last snack on his wrinkled grey wool pants. He hadn't been to his apartment since being rehired, opting to nap under his desk, something many of the lower level staffers did when they were slammed with work.

He stopped typing and sniffed the air, realizing a moment later that the smell of warm stilton cheese was actually him. He hadn't showered in two days.

Between learning the ins-and-outs of his new lower paying job, and keeping McKnight abreast of even the most mundane White House goings on, Lockwood knew he would soon reach his limit. He had to sleep, but he had a job to do. Two jobs, actually.

It wasn't just the work that kept Lockwood from going home, it was also McKnight. At least if he stayed at the White House he couldn't be touched. If he went home, well, he only had so many fingers left and his old college roommate was getting anxious. An anxious Tony McKnight was not good news for Santos Lockwood.

Yawning despite the ample supply of caffeine running through his veins, he cracked his neck from side to side and refocused on the mundane report he was transcribing. Finished, he clicked send and off the document went to the guy who would be taking credit for Lockwood's work.

Closing his word processor, he clicked on a shortcut on his desktop labeled Food Schedule. One of Lockwood's previous duties at the White House had been to assist the kitchen staff in the event that more help was needed, typically when a large group of foreign dignitaries were in attendance.

Over the past year, Lockwood had become friends with the talented cooking staff and their small army of runners. He'd at first volunteered just to get away from his cramped cubicle and because he'd grown up helping his mother, a first generation immigrant from Honduras, in the kitchen as she'd cooked the meals passed down through generations of Honduran women. His father, a former missionary who'd met his mother on a mission trip to Honduras, had always come home raving about his wife's cooking, often throwing a loving wink to his beloved son.

His mother still lived in Texas, but his father had died while twenty-year-old Santos was in college, the victim of a drunk driver. The smell of cooking still reminded him of his dad and the precious meals the three Lockwoods had shared around their modest kitchen table.

He was ashamed to think what he was using his talents for now. His mother would be devastated if she knew. But he didn't have a choice. McKnight had him by the neck, barking commands like he was some kind of slave. The thought made

Lockwood frown until he realized what McKnight would do if he saw his face, so his blank stare returned. He'd perfected it, sensitive to McKnight's mood swings. Lockwood's paranoia was reaching a critical level. Sometimes he felt like the congressman had a secret camera videotaping him 24/7, watching his every move, monitoring his every action.

After perusing the day's meal schedule, Lockwood rose from his desk, peering around cautiously, although he knew no one would be in for at least two hours. That gave him time. After checking to see he had what he needed, he picked up his backpack from underneath his desk and slung it over his shoulder. After another quick look around, he turned for the door and headed toward the White House kitchen.

CHAPTER 29

President Zimmer scooped a spoonful of the brown sugar crust off of the top of his oatmeal. He didn't know how, but one of the chefs had figured out how to make it taste almost like the rim of a crème brûlée, only better. He liked to eat healthy, but allowed himself the small indulgence knowing that he'd need something positive to start the day. *Maybe next time I'll just order the crust.*

Sunlight streamed in from behind, casting a bright glare on his computer screen. He avoided checking his messages, instead reading the day's headlines on a variety of news websites. A voracious reader since childhood, Zimmer skimmed as he ate, casting aside news that he either knew to be false, based on his earlier brief from his national security advisor, or just didn't matter, like the latest splits in Hollywood power couples that some reporter had obscurely tied to politics.

The situation in Lithuania had surprisingly been dropped from headline news, something that deeply concerned the president. Were the American people, and worse, the media,

149

so war-weary they could simply ignore the posturing of a former enemy like Russia? Zimmer thought back to the days after 9/11 when Americans had rallied around their government and taken the fight to the enemy. They were scary times, and yet, had shown the best of what Americans had to offer: grit and determination.

President Zimmer didn't want to go to war, but he'd learned the hard way a strong U.S. military front was all that would keep large and small nations alike from making rash decisions. It was Teddy Roosevelt who'd famously said, "Talk softly and carry a big stick," when describing his view of the American policy. The new president couldn't disagree, only that in certain cases he'd decided it would be better to yell AND carry a big stick.

On the world stage, the United States was still a relatively young nation. Zimmer had no doubt that countries like Russia were waiting patiently for their opportunity to fill the void of one less superpower. The same had happened to countless countries in the past, losing their status as if overnight, including France, Great Britain and Spain, all former mega-powers, now middle players in the global game.

He'd spoken at length with Secretary of State Dryburgh, and the two men were in agreement that the Russian incursion along the Baltic Sea would not go unanswered. Through back channels, they'd dispatched their warning, stating in no uncertain terms that the Americans would not stand by and allow Russia's blatant disregard for international law to go unpunished. The warning shot had been fired and U.S. spy satellites had recorded what looked to be the initial stages of a troop withdrawal. Zimmer didn't want the fight to get ugly, but he was ready should it go so far.

His breakfast finished, Zimmer pushed the empty bowl aside and leaned back in his chair, clasping his hands across his chest. He turned to look out at the brilliant day, watching as Marine guards made their duty changes precisely, not a word being uttered between the Marines who looked to be no more than twenty years old. So entranced was he by the thought that so young a man could be part of such a grand spectacle as the White House, he didn't even hear Travis Haden walk in.

"Mr. President?"

Zimmer swiveled around, still half lost in thought. "Hey, Trav. Sorry, you caught me daydreaming. What's up?"

"I just got a call from General McMillan. He says the Russians are loading their transport ships. He's also gotten confirmation from the CIA, through their local assets. It looks like they're keeping their word. They should be out by midday."

"And we still have Sixth Fleet contingents moving that way?"

"We do."

With the recommendation of the chairman of the Joint Chiefs, his national security advisor, and a loose majority of the cabinet, Zimmer had ok'd the deployment to the Baltic Sea of a small task force from the U.S. Navy's Sixth Fleet, who'd coincidentally been headed that way for a joint training exercise. It seemed that the added pressure had worked.

"I say we let them keep going. What do you think?"

"I agree. It's not the prettiest time of the year over there, but until Russia pulls all their troops out, it's the right thing to do."

Zimmer almost felt like he could breathe a sigh of relief. Southgate was now in their corner and Russia was coming around. Thanks to his team, challenges were being thwarted in an impressive manner. He'd have to bolster their efforts, and get more like-minded, yet conversely talented, members in place. He could think of at least two cabinet members he could replace this second.

"How's Senator Southgate settling in?" asked Zimmer.

"You can tell he's not happy, but he's already got his staff working like a well-oiled machine. I've gotta give it to the guy, when he puts his mind to something, no one's getting in his way."

"That's why he's been around so long, Trav. Let's make sure he feels welcome. I don't want him thinking we hate him. I'm still pissed about what he did, but he can be a powerful ally."

Travis nodded. "Don't worry, I've spread the word. I also told him not to hesitate to ask me if he needs anything."

The olive branch lain with care, Zimmer and his chief advisor moved on to more important topics, namely bolstering the U.S. economy.

Santos Lockwood looked like a recovering alcoholic. Tie askew, wrinkled shirt still showing signs of a coffee sip gone wrong, McKnight's lackey peered through the Waffle House window. He waved when he saw McKnight, who ignored the motion, instead perusing the menu.

The door slammed behind him from the gust of wind that had literally pushed him in the door, customers looking up at the disheveled man in annoyance. He mouthed a silent, *Sorry*.

The diner was almost full, the smell of grease and batter hanging heavy in the air. Luckily the place no longer allowed smoking. Lockwood hated the restaurant chain, but for some reason Tony had always loved the place, despite his attraction to upper-crust establishments. They'd spent countless midday meals, nursing gut-wrenching and head-pounding hangovers, trying to douse the pain with platefuls of meat and carbs, grease and syrup.

McKnight didn't look up as his friend sat down, his ball cap-covered head bowed, staring at his ever-present phone. "What took you so long?"

Lockwood hesitated, knowing that McKnight hated excuses. "A lot of work to catch up on. They've got me doing some—"

"I don't care. I'm having waffles and bacon. Order for me while I go take a piss."

Lockwood nodded subserviently, averting his gaze to pick up the menu, sticky to the touch. He wasn't hungry, at least not around his tormenter.

By the time McKnight returned, Lockwood had placed their orders, he opting for an egg white omelet, hoping to be spared the ribbing about his weight, although his old pal would probably find a way.

McKnight, looking rather pleased with himself for some reason, took a slow sip of his coffee. "So what's new?"

Lockwood shrugged, trying to be nonchalant even though his insides were tangled in knots and he felt like he had to take a dump. "You heard about Southgate?"

McKnight nodded, not wanting to give anything away. Privately, he'd been furious, much like Dryburgh, until he realized that the senator was now probably in a place less likely to do him harm. The congressman had wondered if the senator had mentioned his name to the President, but in the end he didn't care. At the moment, Florida Congressman Antonio McKnight was a nobody. But that was about to change.

"Do you know how it happened?"

Lockwood shook his head, wondering if maybe he should have and that's what the last minute meeting was all about. His knees knocked together twice before he placed a firm hand on each to stop the shaking. "No. It sounded like even Southgate was in the dark. He's busy now, though, doing what he does best, mobilizing his crew like an obedient little army."

"What about Zimmer? How's he doing?"

"I'm not sure. I don't get as much access as…"

McKnight caught himself before he slammed his palm onto the table, gingerly picking up his knife instead, twirling it slowly between his fingers like a drumstick. "I didn't pull those strings and get you back in the White House for you to pull this lame ass shit," he hissed, so only Lockwood could here. "You stay on top of your job or—"

"Isn't what I'm doing enough? I mean, if I get caught they'll throw me in jail, or worse."

McKnight laughed at the look on Lockwood's face. "The only way you get caught is if you run to the president yourself and someone catches you in the act. You're the one who told me you couldn't get caught, right?"

Santos Lockwood silently cursed the day he'd met Tony McKnight. He cursed himself for completing McKnight's assignments so the distracted college student wouldn't fail out of school. He should have let it happen. Hindsight. But at the time, he'd felt sorry for McKnight, whose own father was a drunk, and had spent most of his son's life making him and his mother miserable. College had been McKnight's escape, through a minority scholarship he'd rightfully earned, but the freedom and the memories plagued him. On some level Lockwood had seen himself as his friend's guardian angel. On another, he knew what McKnight might become if given the chance. Lockwood had always been smart, if a bit pudgy and more than a little awkward. The thought of riding McKnight's coattails had been too much for the straight A student to pass up.

"I promise I won't get caught. What I'm doing is untraceable, I told you."

McKnight shook his head. "Sure would be something to see you thrown in prison. I'll bet they'd put you with a big bull…"

Just then the waitress appeared with their food, balanced expertly on a brown serving tray.

"Waffles?" she asked.

McKnight raised his hand and gave her a dazzling smile. Her battle-hardened scowl turned into a broken grin, one that rarely saw the light of day. Lockwood was always amazed at the power his old roommate had over people. It was what made him such a good politician.

"Egg white omelet?" asked the waitress, her scowl returning, as if the mere mention of the healthier fare disgusted her.

Lockwood raised his hand, and their meals were served.

Once the waitress had made her way back to the L-shaped bar, McKnight looked across the table with an evil smirk. "Trying to get healthy on me, Panchito?"

CHAPTER 30

Clouds hung low over the city, obscuring the normally expansive view from The Peninsula Suite. It looked like the weather was going to take another nose dive, the news calling for scattered flurries and more flight delays. What could be seen of the flittering cars below showed the on-again off-again anxiety of New York City winter drivers, always with somewhere to go, but never seeming to get there on time.

Cal, MSgt Trent, Daniel and Leo Martindale had just finished their room service breakfast, the remnants of which now lay in piles on the coffee table.

Due to the obvious security risk should he leave, Leo Martindale had taken Cal's suggestion and stayed the night in their spacious suite. Hotel management had been more than happy to wheel up an extra bed, not that it looked to Cal like Leo had slept. The extra bed was still made to the hotel's exacting standards. He hadn't mentioned it yet, assuming the billionaire was a) scared, and b) always busy.

The mogul didn't talk any more about the murder, pleading to have the night to get some much-needed work done and that they could start investigating in the morning. It wasn't SSI's style, but Cal went along with Martindale's wishes, knowing they'd be able to get more done in the daylight.

"Leo, I'm just curious, how much did this suite cost?"

Martindale didn't look up from his phone. Between that and his laptop, he hadn't stopped working even through breakfast. "Nothing. The owners are friends of mine. I've also done some work for them in the past."

Trent whistled appreciatively. "Sure must be nice to have friends like that. Hell, my boss won't even pick up the tab at the bar sometimes." He flashed Cal a huge grin, receiving a roll of the eyes in response.

Cal turned to Leo, who finally looked up from what he was doing. "Let's go over this again. You got back to your home in the Hamptons two days ago and found your head of security strung up in your garage. Was there any sign of forced entry?"

"No. Even the alarm was still on. Hell, my wife and kids were in the house!"

"How big is the house?"

"Twenty one thousand square feet, give or take a few."

Cal resisted the urge to whistle. Twenty-some thousand square feet was large by anyone's measure. No wonder his family hadn't heard anything. "Did it look like he was killed there or just strung up after they carted in the dead body?"

"If I had to guess, I'd say they did it there."

The air in the room seemed to go cold. None of the men were novices to death, but the fact that someone had been brazen enough to kill the poor guy while the Martindales were but a few feet away sent prickles down Cal's arms. What he wouldn't give to get his hands on the culprits.

"And where's the body now?"

"It's being prepared for the funeral. I was the one who called his wife."

Cal didn't envy the man. He'd had to make similar visits in the past, events that would forever be etched in his memory. "Where's your family now?"

"They're at our place here in the city with round-the-clock security. I'm looking for a place for them for the next few weeks."

That was good. Cal didn't want to have to worry about watching the family too. If he had, it probably would've meant calling in a new team to do that part. "And what about the police? What are they doing to investigate?"

Martindale hesitated for a moment, looking slightly embarrassed, as if wondering how much he should say. "I… pulled a couple strings. I know some guys high up in the department. They understood my need to keep things under the radar. Lucky for me it happened in the Hamptons and not in the city. NYPD probably would've been all over me. Anyway, I told them that I'd like to keep it discreet until I could have my people look into it, citing federal financial law and possible security breaches within our system."

Cal was having a hard time believing the authorities would give Martindale, despite his billions, the latitude to skirt the law. It was turning a blind eye to a heinous crime. "What's the deal you made with them? Obviously they can't just let it go."

"No. They gave me four days."

"And then what?"

"Then they'll take over the investigation, which will be all over the news before you can say bootcamp."

Cal could see why Martindale wouldn't want that to happen. For a man whose business was based on trust and the money of thousands of investors, word of a security breach, let alone the murder of Dale & Moon's security chief, could send clients into a panicked frenzy. Cal looked to Daniel and Trent, who both nodded. "Okay, so where should we start?"

—•—

PARIS, FRANCE

The hotel dining area was packed, each table expertly arranged to maximize the bulging space of the low lit room. Mostly aristocrats, with a smattering of Asian tourists, the diners kept their voices at a comfortable murmur, the sound of soft classical music floating along its edges, piped in from some unseen source.

It felt stifling to Jonas Layton. Preferring the laid back air of open sidewalks and gabby coffee shops, he did his best to keep his cool, focusing instead on his phone and the never-ending influx of messages from around the globe. He had already turned down two European firms who'd done their best to recruit Layton for extended jobs. Citing an ongoing transition back home, he'd expertly maneuvered his way around a flat out no, instead offering a few free tidbits that could help their respective companies immensely, the insight alone probably worth upwards of hundreds of thousands of dollars. The executives had left looking somewhat sad, but Layton knew they were acting. He'd let them off the hook without paying a dime, and had even been kind enough to give them something valuable in return.

Truthfully, Jonas Layton didn't want any more work. He already had enough on his plate, and if the thing with Dryburgh worked, he and his company could be set for quite some time. The thought made him smile, wondering where he'd take his next extended vacation, something he'd instituted for himself five years earlier after a near nervous breakdown.

Now he worked two months and took the third off. He'd found that it kept his mind agile, creative and engaged. Most importantly, it kept his genius brain from tanking like so many other ambitious CEOs who'd crashed and burned after taking a start-up to market. If the world knew the climbing suicide rate of successful CEOs, many of whom were considered rock stars in their respective industries, Layton believed fewer and fewer up-and-comers would seek the stardom of the highest level of the corporate kingdom.

His phone pinged, alerting him through the tiny Bluetooth earpiece he always wore in his ear. It was a stock alert he'd set up the night before. Layton's eyes widened as he pulled up the numbers. *From $50 a share down to $27 in half a day!* He quickly scanned the rest of Dow, looking for similar plunges. Nothing out of the ordinary. *How did they do it?*

Early that morning, Dryburgh had stopped by his room to give Layton the ticker symbol of the stock with a cocky, "Keep an eye on this one." Layton had been confused by the tip, especially after doing a little research into the company. Strong cash reserves. Healthy patent life. No executive turnover. Nothing to indicate any abnormalities.

He didn't get a chance to think on it further as two men approached the table, each looking the clone of the other in their cookie cutter Armani wardrobe, topped off with matching baby blue bow ties. Layton rose to meet his courters, already knowing that he'd deny their invitation, instead ready to focus on whatever Geoffrey Dryburgh was concocting.

CHAPTER 31

The Vice President's quarters were in orderly chaos. Movers and staffers dodged each other as they ran to and fro, some placing antique furniture in areas appointed by Southgate, others coming and going with tasks delegated by the new Vice President. To a visitor it might have looked like a mess, but Southgate was like a veteran conductor, each piece of his orchestra within a flick of his switch or a point of his finger. It was how he liked things and he would never change.

"What's the status on the list of the candidates for the Secretary of Commerce?" Southgate asked, taking notes on a yellow lined legal pad as he'd done for decades.

"We've got the backgrounds done on half of the list and the other should be done within the hour," answered one of his underlings.

"And you made sure it was exactly who I told you to put on the list?"

"Yes, sir." The harried staffer had wondered about the candidates who seemed to be pretty scattered across the spectrum of liberals and conservatives, something he hadn't witnessed during his time with his boss in the Senate.

"Good. Any word from the President?"

"Yes, sir," barked another staffer over the din of hammering as the contractors installed the multitude of pictures being brought from Southgate's former home.

"And?" asked Southgate, slightly annoyed, whether at the answer or the hammering no one could tell.

"He said he'd like for you to start thinking about nominees for attorney general."

Southgate winced. The current attorney general was a friend, a close friend in fact. It had been Southgate who had proffered the man's name to the last president. But it didn't matter. He knew his place. It was a hard pill to swallow, but he was obeying his marching orders from the president and taking an unbiased look at prospective candidates. "Very well, I'll have you a list by the end of the day," he answered, already jotting down candidates he thought might be suitable to Zimmer, the stronger the better.

"Sir, can I ask you a question?" asked one of Southgate's senior aides, a matronly woman who'd been with him for over ten years.

"What is it, Helen?"

Helen hesitated, the others looking at her like she was about to make the biggest mistake of her life. Gulping, she asked, "Sir, we were just wondering why the sudden change? I mean, a lot of these names we're researching now were on your, well, let's just say a couple days ago they weren't on your nice list."

Southgate's hand paused in mid pencil stroke. The gathered men and women held their breaths, having all been present for their fair share of Southgate's infamous outbursts. Slowly, his head rose, a strange thin smile spreading as he focused on Helen.

"I will say this only once, ladies and gentlemen. I am now the Vice President of the United States. I take orders, and may I say willingly, from the President of the United States. If any of you have a problem with that, I suggest you hand in your resignation by the end of the day."

No one said a word. No one moved.

Southgate nodded, and then looked back down at his notes. "Good. Now, where were we?"

THE WHITE HOUSE

President Zimmer looked up from his desk, trying to focus on the ever-present Travis Haden sitting hunched over the piled-high coffee table, another fresh cup of coffee throwing a thin plume of steam into the air. "Is it hot in here?"

Travis looked up. "I'm okay. You want me to turn the air up? I can kill the fire too."

Zimmer wiped his brow with a cotton handkerchief embroidered with the presidential seal. "Maybe. I think I'm coming down with something."

"Want me to call the doctor?"

Shaking his head as he loosened his tie, Zimmer said, "No. I think I'll go for a walk, get some fresh air."

"Want me to come with you?"

Zimmer stood, maybe a little too quickly, because he had to grab the desk to steady himself. He took a shaky breath.

Travis was up and on his way over, concern marked clearly on his face. "Are you okay?"

The President nodded and waved his advisor away with a wan smile. "I'm fine, probably just hungry. Can you check on lunch while I take a quick walk?"

Studying his boss with the practiced eye of someone who'd seen all manner of ailments from malaria to smallpox, Travis asked, "Are you sure you're okay? You lost a good bit of your color a second ago."

Zimmer chuckled. "What are you my mom now? Seriously, I'm fine. Should've had more breakfast and less caffeine." Now looking steady, Zimmer moved to the door. "Make sure they put an extra helping of pecan pie on my plate. I think I deserve it."

Travis waited for his boss to go then left out of the side door, opting to run down to the kitchen instead of call. It might be the only chance he'd have to get any exercise today, a thought that bothered him as he walked past the silent Secret Service agents.

The White House kitchen was a bustle of activity as Travis entered, deftly dodging a chef wheeling in a cart of flour. "Sorry, Mr. Haden."

"No problem. My fault."

Travis looked around for the butler, Lester Miles, one of the only faces he knew. Miles was in the corner, stacking silver domes neatly after wiping them each down with the care of mother tending to her newborn. Travis headed that way, careful to stay out of the heaviest lanes of traffic.

"Hey, Lester."

The former Marine looked up. "Good afternoon, Mr. Haden. Can I get you something?"

"I called down for the president's lunch a few minutes ago. Hadn't seen it so I thought I'd take a walk and grab it myself."

Miles looked annoyed. "I gave your lunch to Mr. Lockwood after handing it to the taster. He said he was headed to the Oval Office to deliver some paperwork and offered to help." Miles looked around the kitchen, soon spotting Santos Lockwood in the opposite corner, facing the opposite direction. "There he is over there."

Travis had met the staffer on more than one occasion, although he hadn't remembered the man's name. Lester and Travis headed to where Lockwood was now bent over, maybe picking something up from the floor. By the time they got to him, he was once again standing and looked to be adjusting the tray holding the president's lunch. Travis noticed the beads of sweat on the hair at the base of Lockwood's neck, his collar partially soaked.

The White House butler tapped Lockwood gently on the shoulder. Lockwood jumped, turning and fumbling with something in his bad hand, the one with the missing fingers, the story of the shark attack already having run its course through the staff grapevine. The item fell to the floor. Travis bent to pick it up, an apology already on the tip of his tongue. Just as his hand reached to grab the tiny paper packet, it looked like an old-fashioned medicine pouch from a pharmacy, Lockwood said, "Oh, I've got that."

With his foot he slid it over and swiftly picked it up. Before he could stand all the way up, Travis's hand clamped down on Lockwood's wrist, immobilizing the man's arm.

He stared at the small white packet for a moment, and then, ever so slowly, raised his gaze to meet the wide-eyed terror in Lockwood's eyes. "You want to tell me just what in the hell this is?"

CHAPTER 32

Santos Lockwood's body shook with the strain, eyes darting left and right, barely noticing the curious looks from the passing kitchen staff. He felt like he was about to lose control of his bowels, but it was his bladder that released, darkening first the crotch of his gray pants, a warm stream running down his left leg and into his shoe.

"Mr. Haden, I…"

Travis Haden gripped harder, making Lockwood flinch. "I said, what the fuck is in this envelope?"

Lester Miles moved closer, clamping a strong hand onto Lockwood's shoulder, squeezing just enough to let the terrified man know he was there.

"I…I…"

In the blink of an eye, Travis grabbed the back of Lockwood's head and slammed the man's face into the metal countertop, knocking the lunch tray to the side and causing half the kitchen staff to turn and look. Just as fast, Travis whipped the dazed man back up. "Lester, help me take Mr. Lockwood to my office."

In the wake of a shocked White House cooking staff, Travis and Miles half carried Lockwood out of the kitchen, Travis having carefully folded the mysterious package, slipping it in his pocket.

By the time they got to the Chief of Staff's office, they had four Secret Service agents in tow. "Stay outside. I'll call you in if we need you."

The lead agent nodded uncomfortably. He knew Haden's background, and had been there when Cal and Daniel saved the President's life, twice, but the thought of any interrogation on White House grounds made the man uneasy. For the moment, he didn't have a choice, not even knowing why Lockwood was being dragged to Travis's office.

Travis kicked his door closed as Miles sat the piss-soaked staffer on the floor, not wanting to stain anything else. Sliding the slim packet out of his pocket, Travis waved it in front of Lockwood's face. The slam into the countertop hadn't done any real damage, only enough to give Lockwood a just-noticeable red welt under his receding hairline. "What is this, Mr. Lockwood?"

Santos Lockwood's mind spun, trying to get a bearing, trying to come up with some excuse. He backed away from the crazed man who'd assaulted him minutes before, scooting himself on his rear until his back was against the wall, his head bumping against the chair railing. How had he been so stupid? He'd waited too long to lace the food, his nerves being so frazzled that the two men in the room had completely taken him by surprise. The lack of real sleep added to the constant stress applied by McKnight through thinly-veiled threats left in their shared Gmail account and calls from Tony's anonymous phone number. Lockwood was a wreck. He knew he'd lost and it showed on his face. "I…it's Atropa."

"What the hell is that?" Travis leveled, his voice showing Lockwood that he better answer correctly thereafter.

It was Lester Miles who answered, his eyes wide. "Atropa belladonna. You might know it as deadly nightshade, Mr. Haden."

Travis was at a momentary loss for words. What was Lockwood even doing handling the President's food? There were too many questions to ask, so he started with something simple. "Why?"

Lockwood squirmed, trying to cover his wet crotch with his suit jacket. "It…it wasn't to do any harm, it was—"

Travis exploded. "You're telling me that you weren't trying to kill the President?" He was now standing over the quivering man, trying to decide if he should beat the truth out of him or…

"It's a special strand," Lockwood blurted, pleading, as if the admission would make them see. "It's not deadly. It just produces certain symptoms…"

"Like what?"

"Like anxiety, confusion, paranoia…"

Travis could not believe what he was hearing. Things suddenly made sense. "How long?"

"How long?" Lockwood squeaked.

"How long have you been doing this?"

"Off and on since a month after he got here."

The comment sobered and incensed both of the men staring down at him, Lester for letting it happen under his watch and Travis for the sheer audacity of the act.

"Was this your idea or did someone put you up to it?" asked Haden.

Lockwood looked up at Travis with eyes that spoke of pain and deceit. He couldn't find the words. His eyes squeezed shut, trying to hold off the tears, but they came anyway, like a torrent, flowing with the power of Lockwood's guilt and shame. The months of sneaking around. The years of being bullied and threatened by his supposed friend. All Travis and Lester could do was watch as the man melted before their eyes. They almost felt sorry for him. Almost.

"I asked you a question. Was this your idea?"

Lockwood shook his head emphatically. "No. I could never do it."

The sobbing continued making it impossible for him to speak. Travis asked again, this time more forcefully. "Who made you do it?"

The sobs turned into full blown body heaves, Lockwood's chin repeatedly hitting his chest, the back of his head banging into the wall. Just as Travis bent closer to smack the man out of his hysteria, the office door swung open. Travis whirled around angrily, on instinct grabbing for where his sidearm usually sat holstered, but it wasn't there. It was the four agents who he'd posted outside, weapons drawn at the sound of the wailing man sitting with his back against the wall.

"Mr. Haden, please back away from Mr. Lockwood," ordered the lead agent.

Travis was incredulous. "I asked *you* to come with *me*, remember? I've got this under control."

"Sir, with all due respect, the United States Secret Service is tasked with the safety and security of—"

"Cut the horseshit," Travis snapped, "Someone is manipulating this man into poisoning the President of the United States. Do you want me to ask how in the hell that happened under your watch?"

The agent stepped closer, his partners mimicking his move, coming farther into the small room. "Sir, I promise you that we will get to the bottom of this. Please let us do our jobs."

Travis wanted to scream at the men from the top of lungs. On two occasions his men, the operators of Stokes Security International, had saved the asses of the Secret Service. He'd been thanked personally by the head of the President's security detail and the director of the Secret Service himself. How the fuck were they trying to say he couldn't handle a guy like Lockwood? The tension remained as he took a few breaths, pushing his temper down, knowing that he was too close to finding out who was behind Lockwood's actions. "Fine, just let me ask him one more question."

The agent shook his head once. "I'm sorry, sir, we'll take him to interrogation and get any information you need. We're happy to keep you in the loop."

It was Lester Miles who broke the stalemate, recognizing the determination on both sides. The last thing anyone needed was to have a feud boil over mere feet from the Oval Office. "Mr. Haden, I know how you feel. I'm right there with you. I let it happen, but I trust these guys to do what's needed. They've done it before. They'll do it now."

Travis's glare never left the men with their weapons drawn, now respectfully aimed down forty-five degrees to the ground. He knew he should've beat the truth out of Lockwood when they'd been in the kitchen, but the stares from the cooks had stayed his hand.

With a final huff, Travis answered. "Take him, but let me know. And I want it recorded."

The agent nodded, holstering his weapon, his companions following suit. In a rush of practiced skill, the four men had the piss and now shit-stained Lockwood, still convulsing with tears, dangling in their combined grasps, each man putting their steel hold on one of his appendages. Lockwood showed no signs of understanding what was happening, not resisting at all.

Once the agents and Lockwood were gone, Travis shut the door and sighed. "How the hell did this happen?" he asked more to himself than to Miles.

"I don't know, sir, but I'd like to officially give you my resignation."

Travis looked up from his thoughts. "What?"

"This was my fault, sir. I'll have one of the other butlers take over my duties and stick around as long as you need me for the investigation."

"What are you talking about, Lester? This wasn't your fault."

Miles shook his head sadly. "Yes, sir, it is. I'm the one that allowed Santos Lockwood to get his hands where they shouldn't have been. It's my fault."

Travis appreciated the former Marine's sense of responsibility, his unyielding honor, but he couldn't let the man torpedo his own career because of the actions of another.

"Lester, if you even mention resigning again, I'll have my cousin and Top Trent pay you a visit in the middle of the night."

Despite the gravity of the situation, Miles grinned. "Thank you, sir."

"Hey, don't thank me yet. This may be just the tip of the iceberg. In a couple days you might be wishing I let you quit."

———

SOUTHAMPTON, NEW YORK

Daniel was driving the Mercedes SUV Martindale had leant them for the trip. Luckily the roads were mostly cleared of snow from the previous weeks' storms. There were still plenty of heaping walls of the asphalt-stained white stuff piled along their path, but the warmer weather was beginning the long awaited melt, sending streams running along the winding roadway.

Leo Martindale's mansion, while huge and impressive in all its stately glory, the view of the Atlantic worth millions alone, was a dead end. Whoever had helped Martindale keep the murder quiet also did a very thorough clean-up job. You could barely make out the edges of where the man's blood had pooled on the brick-paved garage interior.

"What do you guys think? What do we tell Leo?" asked Cal.

"We tell him the truth, that it might be better to have the authorities look into it," suggested Daniel, reiterating the point he'd made minutes after inspecting the property's grounds. There was no sign of forced entry or tampering. No noticeable paths to and from the ten-car garage.

"Did you get anything from Neil?" Trent asked.

"No. He said the company network looks clean, nothing suspicious in the surveillance footage. I told him to keep looking."

They continued down the road, most residents still opting to stay home, leaving the thoroughfares mostly clear. Out of habit, Daniel swept his gaze between the three mirrors, always looking for a tail. As they neared a yellow light, the matte black Cadillac Escalade behind them, its rims the same color and texture as the body, juked left, pulled around them, and sped through the red light. Daniel tried to see inside the passing SUV, but the windows were tinted deeply, probably illegally.

They stopped at the red light at a T intersection, each man doing his own analysis into Martindale's case. There were times to spit out crazy hypotheses, but this wasn't one of them. Something deep was going on and not one of them could come up with a motive. Why go after Martindale's company? Sure, there was the thought that whoever was behind the security chief's murder had gotten pissed that the billionaire was sticking his nose where it didn't belong, but why murder his employees? It didn't make sense and that pissed Cal off.

The stoplight turned green and Daniel quickly got their speed back up to just five MPH over the speed limit. The view really was incredible on Meadow Lane; the wide open Shinnecock Bay to the left and sprawling estates on the right. Daniel could see workers diligently moving around the huge homes, plowing and cleaning, probably an endless job with the untold millions running through the posh town.

He had to stop again as a cable service van pulled out of the next drive, taking its time, the driver looking like he'd dropped his phone. Daniel slowed as they approached the idling vehicle, the driver and passenger now out of the van searching for something on the ground.

"What are they looking for?" asked Trent, straining to see.

Daniel went to shake his head, when suddenly the hair on the back of his neck pricked up. He turned to the right too late. A black SUV, a Cadillac emblem proudly displayed on the grill, barreled their way, much closer than it should have been. Daniel threw the Mercedes in reverse, gunning the gas.

"Hold on!"

Tires spinning against the wet pavement, it felt to all three Marines that they were moving in slow motion, the coming vehicle inching closer, now running off the drive and through the brush lining the road. The impact took their breath away, the airbags deploying in response. Instead of backwards, they were moving sideways, away from the road and into the bay.

CHAPTER 33

Travis couldn't stop pacing. Pretty soon he'd wear a path on his beige carpet, still avoiding the stain where Santos Lockwood had lost control of his bodily functions. He'd instructed Lester Miles to deliver a new plate of food to the President and keep the tainted tray for the investigation. Travis hadn't told Zimmer yet, wanting final confirmation from the Secret Service first.

His desk phone rang shrilly and he rushed to pick it up. "Haden."

"Sir, it's Agent Venti."

"Did you find out?"

"Sir, there was a…a situation."

Travis tried to control his breathing and his temper. "What happened?"

"Mr. Lockwood went into cardiac arrest as we were escorting him to the interrogation room. We did everything we could to revive him, but it looks like his heart gave out."

The only thing Travis could do was grip the edge of his desk until his knuckles went white with the press.

"Sir, are you still there?"

Travis wanted to bite the man's head off, tell him what an idiot he'd been for not listening. Now their only witness was dead, their link lost forever.

"Yes, I'm here. Did he tell you anything before he passed?"

This time it was the agent's turn to pause. "Um, no, sir. He was pretty out of it."

"I assume you're having an autopsy done?"

"Yes, sir."

"Please let me know what you find out."

Without waiting for an answer, Travis hung up the phone. It was time to tell the President.

SOUTHAMPTON, NEW YORK

The Mercedes landed in the recently frozen bay upside down, its occupants struggling to extract themselves from the seat belts. Cal calmly slid the double-edged blade from his wrist holster and through his strapping, careful to keep one hand on the ceiling so he didn't come crashing down. "You guys okay?"

"I'm okay," said Daniel, already searching for the best way out.

"I'm a little banged up, but I'll be fine," said Trent, straining to get his seat belt unlocked from under the deployed side and front airbags.

Freezing cold water rushed in through the crushed right panel of the vehicle, seeming to flow faster as the car settled. They'd already hit the bottom, which luckily wasn't too far down. Cal and Daniel were now crouched on the ceiling trying to gauge the easiest escape route. A moment later Trent, the side of his face bloodied from the collision, his right eye already closed, worked to get upright.

"The electronics already went out. I think we'll have to kick out a window." As usual, Daniel's voice was calm. He'd been through much worse before. It was situations like this that made Cal always glad to have the even-tempered sniper at his side.

"Okay. I say we go through one of these back windows. Top, you think you can get through it?"

Trent grunted as he tried to turn around, his oversized frame packed neatly into the passenger side seat. "I think so, just give me a second."

Cal turned sideways in his seat, facing the window. Needing all the leverage he could get, Cal gripped the driver's seat with one hand and wedged his other into the back seat. He readied himself for the double kick, water already up to his knees. "You guys ready?"

Both men nodded.

"Okay. On three. One. Two. Three."

Cal pulled with his arms and kicked as hard as he could with his legs, forcing the power through his feet. The window folded out and cracked along the bottom edge, which was now the top. Freezing water gushed in, the hole not yet big enough for them to climb through. "One more." Cal braced himself again, crashing against the broken window, willing his entire body to spear through the portal. His effort paid off, but not before the entire vehicle filled with the bone-chilling contents of Shinnecock Bay.

———

Travis pushed into the Oval Office, tie loosened and his coat tucked under his arm. President Zimmer looked up from his lunch. "What took you so long? I thought you were bringing our lunches."

Throwing his suit coat on the red patterned couch, Travis walked to one of the chairs in front of the President's desk and flopped down. "We have a problem."

"Another one?"

Travis nodded. "You know that guy Lockwood, the one who had his fingers bit off by a shark?"

"Yeah. Santos Lockwood, right?"

Travis nodded again. He didn't want to alarm his boss, but he had to tell the truth. "It looks like he was lacing your food with some kind of additive."

Zimmer put down his fork slowly. "What do you mean?"

"He said it was a synthesized strain of the deadly night-shade plant."

"Poisonous?"

"It is in its natural form, but this looks to be a milder mix. I've got a call in to a professor over at Johns Hopkins. My people say that if anyone can give us an accurate reading it's him."

The president sat back in his chair, his heart racing. "What about Lockwood? Do we have him in custody?"

Travis knew this was the part that Zimmer wasn't going to like. "We had him in custody. In fact, I was the one interrogating him."

"What did he say? Why did he do it? Wait. Did you say we *had* him in custody?"

"Technically we still do, but now it's just his body."

Zimmer's eyes went wide. "You didn't..."

Travis almost laughed. "No! We didn't kill him. The guy had a heart attack when the Secret Service took him down for interrogation."

"So what now?"

"The Secret Service is on it. If there was someone coercing Lockwood, I'm sure they'll find out who."

———

Congressman Antonio McKnight checked his secret email account again. Still nothing from Lockwood. He was supposed to have an update by now. He made a note to give his old friend a reminder of what could happen if he didn't comply to the letter.

His plan needed to start seeing results. The formula Lockwood had been gradually feeding to the president had been crafted by a drug manufacturer in Mexico, shipped to a P.O. Box in North Carolina, and picked up by Lockwood around the first of every month. It hadn't been cheap, but according to Lockwood, the symptoms were showing despite the President's attempts to hide them.

McKnight had ordered his stooge to up the dosage, his patience wearing thin, especially after the debacle with now-Vice President Southgate. As far as he knew, everything was going according to plan.

CHAPTER 34

Cal, Daniel and MSgt Trent sat in the back of the baby blue late model Dodge Caravan, the seats now soaked through, the smell of cigarettes and stale coffee matching the general mood in the car.

After extracting themselves from the frigid bay, the three Marines had made their way back to the road, flagging down the first vehicle they saw. It just happened to be a fifty-some year old woman who was getting off her housekeeping shift from a house down the road. It didn't take long, thanks to the soggy hundred dollar bills Cal had taken out of his pocket, to get the woman to agree to drive them to the nearest police station. She said it was on her way.

"You boys okay back there?" she asked in her gravely smoker's voice, hacking at the end of the question.

"Yes, ma'am. Just a little cold, but we'll be fine," answered Cal, wishing the woman would just shut up and drive. He hadn't been so cold since his cold weather training in Bridgeport.

"I've got the heat turned up as much as I can. Hey, you sure you don't want me to take you to the hospital? The big fella looks like he could use a doctor."

Trent's chuckle was much nicer than the thoughts going through Cal's mind. "I'll be fine, ma'am. And don't worry about the seats. We'll pay for any cleaning."

The woman nodded, the smirk on her face saying that she damn well better be paid or hell was a comin'.

Five minutes later, they arrived at the small but obviously well-funded Southampton Village Police Department, the well-tended landscaping just peeking out from its snowy encasement. Cal thanked the cleaning woman and slipped her another three bills through the driver's window. Her cracked smile was ear-to-ear as she did a three point turn and sped on her way, smoke trailing from her minivan.

Cal led the way into the modern police station that looked more like a clinic or a retirement home with its partial stone facade, the green metal roof water trickling steady streams from the melting snow cover. A breeze kicked up behind them, ushering their shivering bodies forward, toward the heat and mounds of paperwork.

———

5:45 P.M.

McKnight's whole body tensed, his office, his sanctuary, suddenly constricting, feeling smaller by the second. He placed his cell phone on the desk, his opposite hand running through his hair, disheveling its precise styling.

Congressman McKnight wordlessly pointed to the door, his secretary slipping out of her chair and heading back to her desk. He didn't know which emotion to hold onto. Sadness? Anger? Grief? Dread?

He replayed the conversation with Santos Lockwood's mother minutes before. She'd gotten a call from the White House saying that her son had suffered a massive heart attack. Sobbing hysterically, the woman he'd called Mama since college, the woman who'd been more of a mother to him than the bitch who'd brought him into the world, poured her grief through the phone line. She kept asking why.

The infinitesimal portion of his soul that still cared about anyone other than himself, a talent he'd forged through the years like a prized two-handed sword, felt for his second mother. He wasn't a complete monster. She'd always been kind to him, always insisting he stop in for a warm meal on the odd occasion that he happened to be in town. Even though he felt for Mama Lockwood, he didn't feel an ounce of guilt over his friend's death. Santos was weak. Who other than a weakling could be so easily manipulated?

No.

McKnight had to gather his thoughts, come up with a plan. He'd been so close. The pieces once again coming together, Lockwood unfortunately being an important pawn in the mix.

Think!

He'd been careful. Nothing tying him to Lockwood except for their history since college. There were countless others in D.C. who could be linked to Lockwood. What angle would investigators attack?

Fuck!

Santos hadn't been the healthiest specimen, but he was in his fucking thirties! How the hell was it possible for him to have a heart attack?

McKnight had promised Mrs. Lockwood that he'd find out what he could and help arrange the shipment of the body back home. "It's the least I can do for my good friend," he'd said.

The recollection made him stop.

Maybe…what if?

McKnight slammed his hand on his thigh, congratulating his quick thinking. He would meet the potential disaster head-on just like the bullies he'd confronted on the streets of Miami as a kid. He remembered one kid, fifteen to little Tony's twelve, a recent immigrant from Cuba, who'd harassed the awkward McKnight every day on the bus, his little gang stealing what little lunch money he had. What his mother had slaved for, possibly whored for.

It had gone on for weeks, until one morning before school he'd grabbed the gun in his father's sock drawer. His old man was passed out, another bender wrecking the family dynamic for the umpteenth time.

He knew enough about pistols to check the chamber and ensure the weapon was fully loaded, counted the rounds. Eight. Tony didn't know what a caliber was, but he knew how to take the safety off, how to aim and pull the trigger. *Squeeze it soft like a titty*, he remembered. He'd silently thanked his grandfather, who'd given him a summer's worth of pistol training during a particularly violent time in the McKnight family. His mother's parents took him in to let his parents try to work out their differences, as if that was going to happen. It was the best summer of his youth. Days of following his grandfather around, eating grandma's food, learning about cars and guns. Yes, he had enough knowledge.

The gun slipped easily into the front pouch of his hand-me-down backpack. Suddenly he wasn't scared, a feeling so foreign it seemed that some heavenly power had pumped his body full of confidence and courage. The pistol stayed in the backpack through the ride to school, through morning classes, through lunch and up until the final bell.

Tony McKnight boarded the bus that afternoon, striding a little longer, walking a little taller. No one noticed, not even his nemesis, the kid that everyone called La Rata, Spanish for The Rat. As soon as the bus started rolling, the harassment began, La Rata and his little gang surrounding Tony, poking him with their dirty fingers, calling him names, laughing at his out of style clothes. "How much money you got?" asked La Rata.

"I don't have any," answered Tony, keeping his stare on the seat in front of him. He'd given up looking to the obese chain-smoking bus driver for help. She'd seen it all and didn't give a shit.

La Rata smacked Tony on the back of the head. "*Mentiroso*," he said. Liar.

"I swear…but I know where I can get you a lot."

The bully's eyes narrowed. He bent lower, whispering in Tony's ear, his breath stale, a hint of weed on its edges. "Whatchu talking about?"

Tony was careful to keep his voice low. "There's a store down the street from my house. I know the combination to the safe."

La Rata knocked his head into Tony's. "How the fuck you know this?"

"I help there on the weekends."

The bully paused to consider the situation just as young Tony had known he would. Bullies loved money, especially the ones with a taste for the good life. La Rata waved his cronies away. They complained but complied, leaving the two schemers alone.

"You take me, now."

Tony nodded. Two more stops until his. He waited, La Rata taking a seat next to him, guarding his prize.

It came sooner than Tony remembered, his hands shaking for the first time that day. "This is my stop."

La Rata got up and motioned for Tony to go first. They stepped off the bus, one after the other, Tony's hearing suddenly masked by the pounding in his ears, adrenaline coursing, nerves raging, palms sweaty, breathing shallow. It took a shove from La Rata for Tony to realize he'd been asked a question, probably more than once. He looked back at his aggressor. "What?"

"I say, how far?"

"Uh, it's right up there." He pointed to the alleyway across the barren street, still too early for the afternoon traffic jams frequented by orange vendors with their shopping carts and the little immigrant boys with their bottles of spray and squeegees.

"Go."

Tony nodded at the order, looking both ways before he crossed, careful to take his time, the plan seeming to unravel in his head. Before he knew it they stepped up to the back door of Kenny's Barber Shop where Tony swept the floors when he wanted to get out of the house. He reached for the door knob that was always unlocked during business hours. "I'll be right back."

Before he could turn the knob, La Rata grabbed him by the collar and turned him around, a switchblade appearing in his hand. How had Tony missed that?

"You better not be lying, *cabrón*." He waved the blade menacingly in front of Tony's wide eyes. "You understand?"

Tony nodded, his tongue dry, his throat caught, his stomach churning. He felt the sudden urge to go to the bathroom.

La Rata pushed him to the door and Tony gratefully opened it, stepping inside. He immediately rested his back against the door, taking breaths like he'd just held it for an hour.

"Tony?"

Tony's eyes popped open at the sound. "Oh, hey Mr. Fuller."

Kenny Fuller, the owner of the barber shop, a black man in his early seventies, hunched from a lifetime of bending over to clip, buzz and shave hair, looked at him quizzically. "I wasn't expecting you today. Everything okay at home?"

Kenny was one of the few people in the neighborhood who knew exactly what Tony was up against with his parents. It was Kenny who'd found Tony sitting on a curb at midnight, rain pouring down, tears long since run dry.

"I'm fine, Mr. Fuller. I just…uh, I thought I left my coat the last time I was here."

"Did you find it?"

"No, sir. I probably left it somewhere else."

"Okay. I'll keep an eye out for it anyway. You still coming by on Saturday?" Kenny asked with a smile, his rheumy eyes squinting.

"Yes, sir. I'll be here."

Kenny Fuller nodded and headed back to work through the curtain that separated the workroom from the break room, leaving Tony to exhale in relief. He waited another two minutes, carefully unzipping his backpack and pocketing the pistol. He pulled his shirt over the butt of the weapon that stuck out.

Saying a quick prayer for no other reason than the added courage, Tony turned and walked out into the alley.

La Rata was waiting, squatting, tracing lines in the cement with his blade. He rose. "You get it?"

Tony nodded, not trusting his voice.

"Give it to me."

"Let's…let's go down there." Tony pointed farther down the alley where a dumpster lay open, a filthy mattress bending over the lip.

La Rata didn't argue. The two boys walked around the random debris littering the pavement, a brown stream running down the seam of the alley. They stepped behind the dumpster, Tony looking around for any observers.

La Rata gave Tony a 'give it to me' gesture. Tony handed over his backpack shakily. It didn't take the bully a moment to search the nearly empty bag and look up. Tony returned the boy's gaze, now holding his father's pistol confidently, pointed straight at La Rata's face.

The Cuban's face blanched. "Whatchu…"

"Shut up." Tony hissed, his voice trembling slightly. "You're not going to bully me anymore."

Before the teen could respond, Tony pulled the trigger three times, every round slamming into La Rata's face, exiting with splashes of brain matter against the far wall. The immigrant fell to the ground, his face unrecognizable.

Tony looked down at the dead boy. For some reason he had the urge to spit in the bully's face, but he resisted, even then understanding the implications of trace evidence thanks to the detective novels he'd read in the library.

After bending down to snatch his backpack, somehow luckily blood free, Tony stashed the gun back in his pocket and took off down the far end of the alley.

It wasn't hard to find a waterway to throw the pistol into, lost forever in the currents frequented by Florida alligators. He walked the rest of the way home, his breathing normal, his mind grasping what he'd done. His elation never bubbled over, young Tony already taking on the mannerisms of a practiced assassin.

Months later they'd traced the rounds in La Rata's death to the gun registered to Evan McKnight, Tony's father. As a convicted felon, on parole, with a history of violence, and the fact that when they'd come to question him he'd attacked the cops in a drug-induced rage, the trial progressed rapidly.

With three shots Tony McKnight had taken care of two problems in his struggling young life. He hadn't planned his father's conviction, but soon understood the power of controlled circumstances. It was the birth of the man who would one day become a United States Congressman.

Just like that day when he'd disposed of the bully, McKnight searched his mind, swiftly coming to the beginnings of a plan. With a nod, he picked up the phone and dialed.

CHAPTER 35

It took hours to file the police report and hitch a ride back into the city. Martindale had thankfully sent a car to pick them up, along with a change of clothes newly purchased from some swanky clothing boutique. Not one of the three recognized the brand.

Now safely back in their suite in the middle of the city, Cal sipped on an oversized tumbler full of Jack Daniels. MSgt Trent was sprawled out on the white couch, with a matching glass, facing the sixty inch television, watching some reality show with catty debutants, sporting a swollen face he'd refused to get checked out except by the EMT-trained cop at the Southampton Police Department. The fireplace held a low flame in the embers that the designer had made to look like aqua crystals, not really providing heat, just scenery.

Daniel walked into the room, having just taken a shower, towel still wrapped around his trim waistline, his blond hair hanging wet just below his shoulders. "Any word from Leo?"

Cal pointed to the phone. "He just called. On his way over. Can you hold down the fort? I need to take *this* drink into *that* hot shower."

"Go ahead. I'll order up some food, too."

Cal's stomach growled at the mention of food. They hadn't eaten since lunch. "Get me a hamburger and fries." With his order in, Cal tromped back to the bathroom, shedding his new clothing as he went.

By the time he got back to the living room, barefoot, dressed in a pair of faded jeans and a white T-shirt, the food was waiting and so was Leo. "Look what the cat dragged in."

Leo stood up. "Cal, I can't tell you how sorry I am for what happened."

Cal waved the apology away. "It's not your fault. Besides, Top is always bragging about what a good swimmer he is. Today he got to try and prove it."

MSgt Trent looked up from his heaping plate of linguini and red sauce. "Try?"

"Top, you almost didn't make it out of the car window." The oversized Marine had not only gotten his shirt caught on the corner of the busted window, he'd also had a helluva time squeezing his large frame through the opening.

Trent shrugged as if just remembering the tiny detail, a peril that would have panicked and killed most men.

"Maybe it was a bad idea bringing you guys up here. I should call the cops and tell them to go on with the investigation," said Leo, his composure from the day before gone, now replaced by panic. "There were two more stock drops today. I think they're building up to something."

Cal sat down and lifted the lid off his dinner, steam rising with the smell of perfectly grilled beef and hand-cut French fries. He savored the sight for a second. "Still no clue who's behind it?"

"No, but I'm starting to think it's more than some tech-savvy brokerage. What would you say if I told you that I think the government may be behind it?"

Everyone looked up at the billionaire. Trent asked the obvious question. "Why?"

Martindale paced around the sofas, gesturing with his hands as he explained. "Is it possible for some hacker to get into the stock market and make some disruptions? Sure. But if that was the case, I'm sure they'd lock down the system if the intruder wasn't purged almost immediately. No, it's got to either be someone who has access to the Dow's back end, or someone's pulling the strings from high up."

"I don't understand. Why couldn't that still be someone who's really connected inside Wall Street?" asked Daniel, forking another bite of just rare enough sockeye salmon.

"It's all in the response. No one's throwing up the red flag or sounding the alarm. I mean, if my company was losing half of its worth in a day, for no apparent reason, you better believe I'd be calling every official I could to get to the bottom of it."

"What if the companies don't want the publicity?" asked Cal.

"It still doesn't make any sense. If company stock takes that big of a hit, the stockholders, especially the big ones, would be in an uproar. It's as if they knew it was coming."

Cal didn't know much about stocks other than the fact that his grandfather had given him ten shares each of Coke and Disney when he was a kid. He'd always let the experts handle his money. "So let's reach out to the companies and see what they say."

"I can't do that."

"Why not? Don't you own some of those stocks with your clients?"

"Sure, but it's not that easy. We've got sort of a code on Wall Street. You don't go looking for a rat unless the damn thing's already caught."

"What the hell does that mean?"

Leo thought about how to explain it better. "Have you ever noticed how celebrities never talk bad about one another?"

"I don't know, maybe."

"It's because Hollywood is too small. All the big names know each other to some degree. Plus, not everyone churns out hit after hit. Even the top actors and bands flop every once in a while. They know that and treat each other with respect even though most of them don't like one another. It's the same thing on Wall Street. Throwing an accusation around is like waging war on your neighbor. You'll never hear the end of it."

Cal thought it was kind of juvenile, but he could understand it. "Okay, so you can't do it, but we can, right?"

"Sure. But you're not getting paid to do that."

"I know. Just call it our patriotic duty. Besides, I wouldn't mind ruffling a few Wall Street feathers."

"Ruffling feathers is what Cal does best," announced Trent.

Leo laughed. "Okay. Tell me what you need."

———

PARIS, FRANCE
8:04 A.M., MARCH 8TH

Jonas Layton strolled through the nearly empty park, a sole bum, braver than his friends, lay on a pile of cardboard on the stone pavement, covered in a mound of old bedding. A thin line of steaming breath the only sign that the man was still alive.

The breeze made the thirty degree weather feel like the negatives, Layton keeping his collar cinched tight. The park was probably half the size of a baseball field, scattered trees looked like haunting ghouls, ice clinging to their branches, bending them in unnatural positions. The American shifted the Yankees ball cap on his head, scanning carefully behind his Persol sunglasses.

He was being watched and he'd already caught glimpses of figures on the periphery. They were being cautious, careful. What did they want? Layton rarely travelled without security, but he'd taken the Secretary of State's assurance that he'd be well protected under his own umbrella. The problem was, he no longer trusted Dryburgh. The American diplomat had asked to meet later in the day, but Layton told his friend he would be leaving on a noon flight back to the States. It was past time to go.

As he made his way to the far exit, where two looming sculptures of long-forgotten heroes stood facing away from the park, Layton could feel the convergence of multiple contacts on his highly tuned radar. Hyper observant, he tracked a knitted cap to the left, a pair of brown loafers to the right, the sounds of faint shuffles behind. He picked up his pace, thinking to make the stoned entrance before the others. Too late, they paced his strides as if in sync.

Fear crept up his back like a troop of stringy-legged spiders. Layton's pulse quickened, pupils dilated, but he kept his hands stuffed in his pockets, carefully measuring the distance to freedom.

As he passed through the exit, two men approached from his left and right, a quick peripheral glance pinpointing the black weapons hanging at their sides.

"Mr. Layton, we'd like to have a word with you," said the man on the right in heavily accented English. French for sure. He wore a brown checkered knit cap over a head that Layton assumed to be bald, dark piercing eyes a mismatch to his smiling mouth. Probably just over six feet tall, the man's muscular physique was evident even under the layers of wool and cotton.

"I'm sorry, what is this about?" asked Layton, trying to keep his voice steady as he clenched his fists inside their protective cocoons.

"Monsieur, we can't say here, but it is a matter of national security."

If he hadn't been so scared he would have laughed. National security seemed to be the excuse for any and all nefarious actions around the world. "I have a plane to catch."

The man to his right had closed in and stood watching, his black overcoat swaying with the breeze, no smile on his face, just the cold stare of a professional used to violence.

"That won't be possible, monsieur. We will be happy to book you another."

"Gentlemen, I suggest you contact my attorney if you'd like a word. Now, if you'll excuse me." Layton stepped off the curb, careful to avoid a divot full of slush. He felt an iron grip on his right arm and stopped, blood pumping faster, adrenaline kicking.

As if on cue, four nondescript French sedans came tearing from different directions, lights flashing red and blue, no sirens. The two men looked up in surprise, the one holding Layton loosening his grip slightly. In the next five seconds no less than ten men, all dressed in impeccably tailored suits, jumped out of the vehicles and started yelling at the two strangers in French to drop their weapons and get on the ground. They did as they were told, weapons first, followed by their slow descent to the ground with hands raised.

Layton breathed a sigh of relief as they were cuffed and thrown into the waiting cars, both men glaring angrily at their intended target. The smallest of the ten men to arrive stepped up to Layton. "Are you well, Jonas?"

Layton nodded. "I wasn't sure you guys were watching."

The man shrugged, doing a funny twitch with his bushy mustache. "You know how we work, Jonas. Always watching."

"Thank you, Lucas. I owe you one."

Lucas shrugged as if what they'd done was nothing. "We will have a talk with these men and let you know what we find out. Now, may I offer you a ride to the airport? Your bags are in my trunk."

"That would be great, thanks." Layton followed the French intelligence chief to his car, grateful that he'd given Lucas a little help a year before with an issue that had plagued his service for months, but which Layton had cracked in minutes.

"I forgot to tell you. The men watching you from the other side of the park have also been apprehended and are on their way to interrogation as well."

Layton shook his head, ever amazed by the seamless expertise of true professionals.

CHAPTER 36

President Zimmer had been at it for over an hour, signed and sealed bills and intelligence reports stacked neatly in his OUT box. Despite the events of the day before, he felt rejuvenated. Preliminary reports from Johns Hopkins suggested the drug he'd been given had been manufactured specifically to induce stress, fatigue and possibly hallucinations at the right dosage. They wouldn't know for sure until they'd done some more testing, but the doctor told the president with near certainty that any lingering effects should be out of his body in the next twenty-four to forty-eight hours.

So many things made sense after that revelation. The paranoia, the high blood pressure, the nerves he'd never felt before. Zimmer had privately thought that maybe the office of president was just too big for him, a task he was unworthy of. There were days when he'd barely kept it together, like when he'd offered the positions to Travis Haden and Marge Haines. That had been one of the lows and he mentioned it to Travis. His loyal Chief of Staff had agreed with the assessment, even telling his boss about the concerns he'd had about taking the job due to Zimmer's weakened state.

Even though the symptoms might not have been fully purged, Zimmer felt stronger just knowing it wasn't him, that it had been something else influencing his body and mind. But that still left issues unresolved. Who had put Santos Lockwood up to it? Travis suggested they ask Southgate, what with his recent attempt to capsize the president. The list was short, but had the potential of growing exponentially should they let their imaginations run wild. Any president, no matter how popular, had any number of enemies, mostly unseen, seeking to discredit his legitimacy.

As he was signing yet another letter to a foreign leader, this one to the ambassador of Ghana, his desktop phone rang. By the flashing light he could tell it was his ever efficient secretary. He pressed the speaker button.

"Mr. President, I hate to disturb you, but I have Congressman McKnight on the phone. He said it was urgent."

Zimmer knew McKnight from his time in The House. They'd been in the same freshman class of representatives. He didn't know McKnight personally, but he'd seen the way the young Floridian was being groomed by the Republican Party to be one of its up-and-coming leaders.

"Did he say what he wants?"

"Yes, sir, he says it's about Mr. Lockwood."

Other than Travis, Lester Miles, the president and the Secret Service, the rest of the White House staff was told that Lockwood died of a massive heart attack. It wasn't the whole truth, but until the investigation into Lockwood's co-conspirators concluded, no one needed to know anything but the fact that he died of natural causes. Zimmer wondered how in the hell McKnight had heard about it.

"Did he say what specifically?"

"Yes, sir. Apparently Congressman McKnight and Mr. Lockwood were roommates in college and he's calling on behalf of Mr. Lockwood's family."

That surprised Zimmer. Other than their Hispanic heritage, Lockwood and McKnight were polar opposites. Hell, one was a Democrat and the other was a very right leaning conservative.

"Put him through please, Ellen."

Zimmer waited for the proper number of clicks to sound. "Good morning, Tony," Zimmer said warmly.

"Good morning, Mr. President. I hope I didn't interrupt anything."

"No, not at all. Just the usual pile of nonsense."

McKnight laughed dutifully. "I assume your secretary told you why I'm calling?"

"Something about Santos Lockwood?"

"Yes, sir. We were friends, roommates actually, at Florida State."

"I'm very sorry for your loss. I just heard about it."

"Thank you, Mr. President. I'm also very close with his mother. She was sort of, well, my mom and dad were never around and Mr. and Mrs. Lockwood sort of adopted me in college. Mrs. Lockwood is very upset, as you can imagine, and wants the body sent home as soon as possible. She's getting some pushback from the Secret Service and asked if I could help. I didn't promise anything, but I told her I'd look into it. I've called the Secret Service, got passed around a couple times until I told them who I was, and they told me it's normal procedure that they do a full autopsy. Something about dying in the White House. It sounded, well, like an official statement when they can't really say what's going on. Is there something they're not telling me?"

The president didn't know how to respond. He shouldn't say anything, but he felt for Lockwood's mother. "I'm sure it's just policy, like they said."

"I understand." McKnight was silent for a moment, and then said, "Mr. President, could you do me one more favor?"

"Name it."

"If you hear anything, would you mind having someone give me a heads-up? If Santos was up to anything, I'd like to soften the blow with his mom if I can."

"I will."

"Thank you, Mr. President. One last thing, if you don't mind me saying, you're doing a helluva job given the situation. I know we're supposed to be on opposite teams, but I'd like to say that I'm here to help if you ever need me."

"I appreciate that, Tony. I'll definitely keep you in mind. Have a good day."

Zimmer replaced the phone in its cradle. He wondered if there could be any connection between McKnight and Lockwood's attempt to influence the presidency. He'd have to mention it to Travis and let him run it down. Like most of his daily conversations, the busy president put his latest out of his mind, and got back to work.

Tony McKnight replayed the conversation with the President. He'd practiced what he wanted to say and Zimmer acted predictably, even telling McKnight without outright saying that the Secret Service was investigating Santos. The congressman had to be careful, but he was confident of his abilities. He was confident that not a shred of evidence existed to implicate him with Lockwood's scheme. There'd been numerous middle men who'd provided the doctored drug Lockwood gave the president. The plan had worked to perfection up until his untimely death.

A friend of a friend had one day mentioned to McKnight on a trip overseas that a former Russian scientist was making millions on the underground medical market by supplying various criminal organizations with undetectable poisons made from common plants readily found around the world. Poison was older than human kind, and had been used for centuries as an effective tool. There was something poetic about its beauty, McKnight thought.

He'd had Lockwood track down the scientist's organization and put in several small orders through American small businesses who were only too happy to take delivery of the tiny packages and forward them on to P.O. Boxes in Virginia and Maryland. Never once had McKnight had direct contact with any of the packages or contacts. He did, however, have all the information should the need arise to let someone else take the fall.

Making his mind up, he began laying down plans for the official unveiling. He had just the person in mind to become his scapegoat.

CHAPTER 37

They'd separated the five mercenaries into different cells. The first hour was spent with polite questioning, Lucas doing most of the talking, as the stripped down mercenaries refused to talk. It was obvious that these men were trained to take interrogation, silent across the board. But Lucas was a professional, a patient man, a former spy turned protector of France. He'd spent the last ten years battling the influx of Middle Easterners looking to turn his country into another haven for smugglers and terrorists. Lucas despised most of the citizenry of France, too consumed with touting the superiority of French cuisine or railing against the Americans to see that their beloved country was growing a cancer which could no longer be walled off with concrete.

By the second hour, Lucas knew that three out of the five men were muscle and nothing more, paid to give the crew some added firepower. After the fingerprinting came back, they found that all five men were former French Foreign Legionaries, a revelation that didn't surprise Lucas, who in his late teens and early twenties had spent five years with the famous commandos. As was common in specialized military branches around the world, many Legionaries went on to have extended careers in private security companies, only retiring when they were too old to keep up, or too dead to care.

The leader of the small band, the eloquent man who'd spoken to Jonas Layton, went by the name Taureau, which in French means *bull*. His real name was Alexandre Fortier, and after some digging, and a phone call with an old comrade, Lucas found out that Fortier was employed by a quickly growing French security company called Sécurité Lion International. Lucas knew the outfit to be tight-lipped and any phone call he made would most assuredly go unanswered. The company was a constant thorn in law enforcement's side, having already been implicated in half a dozen shoot-outs that year.

To Lucas they were no better than common thugs, although this Fortier fellow seemed to be one of the exceptions, his blue eyes scanning carefully, thoughtfully, not a hint of rage like the others. Lucas sat across the heavily scratched metal table from Fortier, whose hands were shackled to the bolted steel chair, making him lean down every time he took a drag from his unfiltered Gauloises cigarette.

The microphones and video cameras kept rolling as Lucas waited patiently, looking for any sign that the man wanted to talk. None came. "Tell me, Taureau, what did you want with Mr. Layton?"

Fortier shrugged, cracking his thick neck from side to side. "I told you, I was only given orders to escort him."

"Yes, yes, I forgot. And who did you say hired you?"

Another lazy shrug. "I didn't because I don't know. Why don't you call my boss?"

Lucas chuckled. "You know as well as I do that your employer will never take my call unless we have a warrant from the government. Now, while I could do that, and have you sit in a cell as those wretched bureaucrats decide which one will steal the credit for taking your company down, I'd much rather handle this between us, two old Legionaries, eh?"

"You were in the Legion?"

"Oui."

"You're pretty small."

Lucas smiled. "I had my talents. I still do."

Fortier took another drag from his cigarette, sizing up Lucas for the first time. "You know I can't say anything."

"I know. Look, I'm happy to look the other way, and call this a, well, we won't call it anything. I'm sure your employer will be upset enough about you not completing the job. Wouldn't he be even more upset to find out that we picked you up?"

Fortier didn't answer, but Lucas knew the truth. As the team leader, Fortier would more than likely take the heat, maybe even have to pay a penalty out of his own paycheck. Such men rarely parted with their money easily.

"Alex, all I need is to know where you were taking Mr. Layton. Tell me that to my satisfaction, and I will let you go, I'll even destroy the paperwork."

"And why would you do that? Just a favor for a fellow Legionnaire?"

"Unfortunately, no. Let us simply say that Mr. Layton is a very good friend of my employer and of our government.

They would be very unhappy to find out that you and your company were involved in harming such a good friend."

Fortier's eyes darted briefly, the first hint of nerves he had shown. He looked up at the video camera, motioning with his eyes.

"Perhaps we should have this conversation in a more private location, say my office?"

"And you'll destroy the footage you've already taken."

"You can watch me do it."

Fortier nodded.

———◆———

Jonas Layton was halfway across the Atlantic, stretched back in his roomy white leather lounger in first class, reading the latest edition of *Fast Company* when his phone rang. "Lucas?"

"Hello, my friend. I take it you're flying home comfortably?"

"Yes, thanks to you."

"Ah well, it was an easy thing to do for someone to which we owe so much. Can we speak on this line?"

"It's fully encrypted."

"Good. I found out where they were taking you, but not why."

"Where?" Layton put a finger to his lips, wondering if his hunch had been right.

"You were first to be transported to your hotel to retrieve your belongings and then driven to a villa outside Reims."

"Did they say who hired them?"

"The man in charge of the team mentioned overhearing his employer talking to someone on speakerphone who was obviously an American. He thought he heard the name Geoffrey. Does that help?"

Layton entire body went rigid. He'd had his suspicions, but this was too much to ignore. "It does. Thank you, Lucas. Please let me know if there's anything I can do to return the favor."

"Completely unnecessary, my friend. Let me know if I can be of further assistance."

Layton ended the call and pressed the button for the flight attendant. A pretty brunette in knee high stockings and a blue skirt suit that perfectly contoured her body walked down the aisle and asked how she could help.

"A double whiskey on the rocks, please. No, make that straight up."

The stewardess nodded and left to fetch his drink. Jonas Layton looked up at the white ceiling and thought about who he could ask for help.

CHAPTER 38

"You took care of it?"

"I did."

"And you did like I told you, hard to find, but not too hard?"

"Come on, pal, I know what I'm doing, okay?"

"I know. Just making sure. I'm wiring you the funds now."

"Cool. Let me know if you need anything else."

Congressman McKnight removed the voice modulator from the pay-as-you-go phone, pocketing the modulator and throwing the cell in the construction dumpster being used near the Washington Monument as he walked. He smiled, his eyes gleaming behind black Gucci sunglasses. It was so easy to find good, cheap help.

The Secret Service investigator sat in what he wouldn't even call a bedroom. One larger room was crudely cut into four by wire strung curtains, typical of low-paid government workers living in the city. There was a mussed single mattress, clothes thrown haphazardly around the curtained off space. Luckily he'd brought a camp stool and sat on it as he pecked away at the laptop belonging to the now deceased Santos Lockwood. All the recent files seemed harmless. Another team would go into greater depth later. He was there to get immediate results.

There hadn't been much security to keep him from nosing around until he found a file marked NMP stashed in a random location with copied internet articles. He double clicked the folder and a password screen popped up. Rather than lock himself out, he pulled a thumb drive out of his pocket and plugged it into the computer's USB drive. The connection registered on the screen and he waited for his personal icon to appear, a parrot wearing a skull t-shirt. As soon as it did, he clicked and dragged the parrot, repositioned it over the locked file and released. The little icon pecked away as it worked, circumventing the protocol in less than a minute.

The file opened and the front line hacker quickly sorted through the jumble, the pointer soon hovering over an unnamed file. He double-clicked it. A moment later, his eyes went wide.

"Hey, Jake," he said over his shoulder, "I think you better come take a look at this."

PARIS, FRANCE

Geoffrey Dryburgh was about to blow his lid. Those Lion Security idiots had lost Jonas Layton, and no one could seem to find him. "How on God's green Earth could your men not find one pathetic little computer geek?"

Dryburgh listened to the excuse from the CEO of the company he'd hired to dispose of Layton. He never should have included the genius, should've known he'd go snooping around. That was just his nature. Rather than blame himself, something he never did, Dryburgh railed against the security contractor, who only knew him as a foreigner named Geoffrey. "You're not getting a fucking penny from me, and you better return my goddamn deposit today. We'll see if you ever hear from me again."

Dryburgh slammed the secure phone down, hoping he'd break it, but just causing the receiver to fall off the cradle. He stared at it angrily, breathing in and out like a raging bull. Something had to be done, but what?

A crazy idea popped into his head a moment later, his crisis management mode enabled. He picked up the phone again. Referencing a small green notebook he always kept in his right pants pocket, he dialed a number and waited for the pickup.

"Hello?" came the bored answer.

"Igor, it's Geoff. We need to talk."

———

THE WHITE HOUSE

Agent Brett Stayer stepped into the Oval Office, his appearance so common that none of the three men looked up when he entered. "Excuse me, Mr. President."

Zimmer glanced up from where he sat deep in conversation with Travis and Gen. McMillan. "What's up, Brett?"

"Sir, we have an update on the investigation."

The president and Travis both looked at McMillan. "Would you like me to leave for a moment, Mr. President?" asked the chairman of the Joint Chiefs.

Zimmer thought it over. While he didn't want it getting around that someone had been poisoning him, a fact that he and Travis planned to keep quiet, who better to tell than a Marine four-star whom he trusted completely? To help make the decision, Travis nodded his assent.

The President turned to McMillan. "General, we've recently uncovered a plot to, well, I guess you'd say poison me."

The normally unflappable Marine's face went red and he almost stood up, as if going for his sword to protect the king. "What? How did that happen?"

"Long story short, it was someone in the White House, who is now dead, but it looks like we may have a lead. Brett?"

"Yes, sir. The team that went over to Lockwood's apartment found something on his laptop. Mr. Lockwood was possibly coerced by a former Russian scientist now living in Brazil. We found copied emails and shipment reports between Lockwood and the Russian's organization detailing the threats to Lockwood's person and family, along with the particulars on where the drug would be sent, and how it should be administered over time."

"A Russian?" asked Travis.

"Yes, sir. We're working with the CIA and FBI to see if there's any connection with the Russian government."

President Zimmer couldn't believe it. First the affair in Lithuania and now they were trying to poison him? It sounded like something out of the Dark Ages. "Who else knows about this?"

"Our people and you three. We didn't tell the other agencies what the query was about, only that we needed it ASAP."

"Since we've got you here, General, what are your thoughts?"

Gen. McMillan took an extended moment to respond, obviously weighing every angle like a commander evaluating the battlefield. "Sir, the Russians do have a history of this sort of thing. Remember the ex-FSB officer, Alexander Litvinenko? He's the guy that fled Russia and got asylum in the UK."

Zimmer did remember. "Right. He was the one they allegedly poisoned with radioactive material."

"Yes, sir. Polonium-210, if I remember correctly."

"And let's not forget all the poisoning the Greeks and the Romans did. Jeez, are we going back to that?"

"I wouldn't put it past them, Mr. President."

CHAPTER 39

Cold calling companies had been a complete waste of time. The second the company got a whiff of what Cal and his friends were after, they retreated inward like a Greek phalanx. Most directed their inquiries to investor relations, another dead end.

The team of four, including Leo Martindale, who would occasionally step into another room to take a call, had been over and over different scenarios, the three whiteboards one of Leo's assistants had delivered being the proof. Lines, notes and scribbles intertwined for a web that would make a spider dizzy. After close to four hours of investigating, they were no closer to the answer. Each company was unique, rarely sharing more than a pinch of similarity with another corporation whose stock had tanked and then recovered. How did a textile company relate to a pharmaceutical company? Or a natural juice company and a healthcare software company? It didn't make any sense.

To make matters worse, there was no evidence of insider trading, no major stockholders moving in to take advantage of the stock plunge by short selling or selling to avoid a larger loss. It all seemed too coordinated and yet completely ignored. Not even SSI's resident genius Neil Patel could establish a pattern.

Cal stood up from the grey leather armchair and stretched, trying to piece it all together as his eyes bounced from white board to white board. What the hell was going on?

THE WHITE HOUSE

"Sir, I have the Secretary of State on the phone," came Ellen's voice through the speaker phone.

"Patch him through, please."

"Mr. President?" Dryburgh asked, his voice sounding rushed.

"I'm here, Geoff. Are you on your way back from Paris?"

"Yes, sir."

"Good, I have some things I need to run by you. What's—"

"Sir, I have some news."

Zimmer took a deep breath. "What is it?"

Dryburgh didn't answer immediately. "It's the Russians."

The president sat up in his chair. "What now?"

"Sir, I don't know how to say this. I just got a call from them."

"And?"

"They said they're calling our debt."

Zimmer was confused. Dryburgh couldn't be talking about the U.S. investments held by every major country in the world, the standard for modern currency. "What do you mean they're calling our debt?"

"They say we have seventy-two hours to pay back every penny we owe."

———————

Neil Patel loved a good puzzle. As a child his father had given him daily riddles to solve. That had progressed to mathematical equations and questions with no right answers. Neil was used to the unknown, used to bending the rules to make something work, to see how something ticked.

The stock manipulation was something else entirely. He'd looked at it from twenty different angles, trying to make sense of it all, but so far he couldn't. His team had meticulously tracked every trade to see if they could find some correlation between the trader and the resulting drop in stock price. They'd sifted through reams of news searching for any little scrap that could explain it. Nothing.

Neil knew most people thought the stock market was like going to Vegas and putting fifty bucks on red, but he knew better. The entire system was highly complicated, yet prone to the rise and fall connected to national emergencies, war or even public sentiment. Hell, there'd been more than one stock that had skyrocketed because their YouTube video raked in millions of views in a single day. It was easy for people to dismiss the stability of the market because of such outcomes, but in the end, as long as whatever had precipitated the change went away, the stock price would level out. That was the reason most financial advisors told their clients to take a long-term approach to investing instead of tracking it day-to-day.

But the stock market was still the stock market. It could be manipulated in subtle ways, but Neil had only heard of rare cases where a stock was so completely controlled like the twenty seven they were tracking. It aggravated the tech genius, not because someone was doing it, but because he couldn't figure out how.

He reached under his desk to where he'd installed a mini fridge, opened it and pulled out another diet energy drink. It was going to be a long day.

The president called in Travis and gave him the news. After standing in shock, Travis suggested they call in the necessary cabinet members. They'd arrived within the hour, disturbed by the urgency of the request.

The Situation Room buzzed with nervous energy, some sipping coffee, others simply waiting for the President to speak. They'd learned quickly that Zimmer was not a man to mince words. If he had something to say, he'd say it.

When the last cabinet member arrived and took her seat, the President spoke. "Ladies and gentlemen, just over an hour ago I received a call from Secretary Dryburgh, who is now on his way back from Europe. He'd just gotten a call from the Russians. It seems that they've got their panties in a wad over something. Long story short, they, along with four other countries, are cashing in their U.S. investments."

As expected, half the room exploded in questions, some sat in shock. The President held up his hand. "Let go around the room one at a time. Let's start with treasury."

The Secretary of Treasury's face was red and he could barely put the words together, so flustered was he by the President's revelation. "Mr. President, do we know why they're doing this? I mean, they know what this will do to the global market. Every currency in the world will be affected. It's suicide."

"We haven't been able to reach the Russians. It looks like they're hunkering down for the time being."

"Sir, if this gets out, we'll probably have to shut down the stock market."

Zimmer knew that was right where the treasury secretary would go. It was true. If even a whisper of U.S. debt being called made it into mainstream, or even not so mainstream, news, the effects could be devastating. Not only would Wall Street take a hit, everyday Americans could see their retirement savings wiped out.

"I know. Let's hope it doesn't get to that point. Does anyone have any ideas of why the Russians would do this?"

"They've been hinting at some huge oil and gold reserve they found a couple years ago," offered the peevish Secretary of Commerce. "Maybe they think they're strong enough to stand on their own."

The President shook his head. "That wouldn't make any sense. They're not North Korea. They'll be affected by this too, no matter what they think. They're part of the global economy."

"What about the situation in Lithuania, sir?" asked the Interior Secretary, an old cowboy who sported the weathered

look of the original Marlboro man. "Could this be in retalia-
tion to the action we took to get them out?"

"I just don't know. Until we get someone on the phone
from Moscow, we're just guessing." More murmurs around
the room. "I need you all to handle this delicately, no leaks.
Let's try to find out why they're doing this, and if they go
through with it, what the impact will be on us. I want a plan
in place before this inevitably hits the airwaves. Let's not get
stuck with our pants down, people."

With the meeting officially ended, every department
head rushed to start their confidential inquiries. Travis
watched them go, the President taking notes on a yellow lined
legal pad. He was proud of Zimmer. His body and mind were
getting back to where they should be after Lockwood's coercion, and aside from the initial shock from Dryburgh's call,
Zimmer had conducted himself as a president should.

Travis knew that with Zimmer's confidence on the rise,
they would have a much better chance of sticking it to the
damn Russians.

CHAPTER 40

Every window in the one bedroom loft was covered, only the occasional ray of light seeping in from a rustling curtain. The air was a precise sixty eight degrees, the smell of orange peel floating through the space from the small burning William Sonoma candle sitting on the rarely used black granite kitchen countertop.

Jonas Layton hadn't left the kitchen table since he'd arrived at his private retreat earlier that day. He didn't want to take the chance that someone would be waiting for him at either his place in Denver, his beach house in Florida, or his penthouse in New York City. His current girlfriend, a six-foot model from Finland, was still on the road, and he had the key to her place. It would be hard to track him to where he sat clacking away, searching.

He'd left his cell phone on the airplane, tucking it into the waste basket in the restroom. Who knew if he was being tracked? He couldn't take that chance. Cell phones were becoming the world's easiest way to snoop on people.

Computers were a different matter. He always carried his custom built laptop, something an old friend did for him at least once a year. It had the ability to remain hidden, all public protocol constantly changing. To anyone searching for him, it looked like just another one of the millions of residential models used around the world.

Layton had started putting the pieces together. His specialty wasn't hacking. His specialty was using everyday information that was readily available on the Internet to make his predictions. Most fans thought Layton had some kind of super-secret program he used to dig into encrypted databases and compile troves of classified information. How else could he be right time after time?

But that wasn't his secret. The key to everything he did, and this included the companies he'd built with his own two hands, was the use of tools available to everyone. He'd learned the lesson from his grandfather, a first generation immigrant from Poland. He used to tell young Jonas that if he couldn't build a house with simple tools, it wasn't worth building. It was a philosophy built on simplicity and the thought that a community could band together and do most anything. The old Jews all had that mentality, many of whom, just like his grandfather, had been through the most harrowing trials during their Nazi concentration camp incarcerations. They'd learned to make tools out of wire, wood and bone. They'd taught each other how to make bread out of scraps, always putting together enough to celebrate the Sabbath.

And so, when it came time for Jonas to go out into the world, he was better equipped than his peers. He learned how to use public information to determine the success of a company or predict the outcome of a marketing campaign.

Instead of looking at the face value of something, he would look deeper and find the meaning behind the action.

When asked, Layton always explained his general method, and yet, no one seemed to believe him, still betting on the fact that he had something up his sleeve, like a practiced fortune teller flipping Tarot cards. One time, when presenting in front of a skeptical group of MIT students, a student had raised his hand and asked him point blank how he did it.

Layton had smiled, knowing the kid wouldn't like his answer. "You know what I've said before, many times, in fact. But the truth is, it's like having my hand on the pulse of every human being on earth. By studying that pulse, by empathizing with their emotions, needs and actions, I'm able to make my predictions." He could tell by the disappointed look on the student's face that it hadn't been what he'd wanted to hear, hoping that he'd have something more concrete to walk away with. But the answer had been the truth. Even now, as he sat scrolling through website after website, he felt the pulse throbbing, telling him something. So close, yet still not there. *Just a little more time.*

President Zimmer stood in the Oval Office, staring off into the peacefully clear night, watching the slowly blinking lights of aircraft waiting for final clearance, or flying to destinations unknown. With the weather having subsided, it seemed as though the airlines and airports all along the east coast were double-loading the number of flights coming in and out.

Zimmer was dressed down, wearing now dry work-out pants and a T-shirt, having hit the small gym thinking that any sweating could help purge his body of the lingering effects of Lockwood's potion. The Secret Service was still working on the Russian scientist lead. Initial inquiries pointed to a possible working relationship with the Russian government.

There was a knock at the door and Travis stepped in, followed by a slightly disheveled Geoffrey Dryburgh. "I'm sorry for my appearance, Mr. President."

"Don't worry about it. Thanks for coming. Can I have the staff bring up some coffee?"

"If it's all the same, I think I'll hold off. I'd like to get a couple hours of sleep tonight."

The President nodded and ushered his guests to the couches in front of the dwindling fire. "Anything more from the Russians?" Dryburgh, or one of his staff, had spent the afternoon sending updates to the President. The Russians were playing hardball, calling their actions an economic play, saying that the U.S. dollar wasn't what it used to be and suggesting that an alternative currency be used as a global standard. It was the same rhetoric they'd been spouting since dragging their communist asses out of their post-Gorbachev downward spiral.

"They're still putting us off. I haven't been able to get one damn person on the phone that wasn't some assistant."

"What's their play, Geoff? Why the sudden revelation and how the hell did they get the other countries on board?" It had quickly come to light that Russia had somehow convinced

Brazil, Belgium and Luxembourg to cash-in their U.S. debt as well. The fourth country was still unidentified.

Dryburgh shrugged, exhaustion clear in his body language. "If you'll excuse the language, these Russians are fucking crazy. They've got a little bit of money again and they think they can start pushing people around. It's like a bully who just got released from the hospital; he's got all this pent up aggression and energy and he's ready to use it."

"Come on, Mr. Secretary," said Travis, "This one came way out of left field. We've known for years they had their eyes on Ukraine and the Baltic. In my opinion, it was only a matter of time. But this? They're shooting themselves in the foot by devaluing our currency."

Dryburgh didn't disagree. "There's more."

The president scowled. "Now what?"

Dryburgh exhaled. "As I pulled up, I got a call from a highly placed contact in the Chinese government. It looks like they may be jumping in with the Russians."

Jonas Layton knew he was taking a chance, but he had to try. His efforts had been fruitless so far, nothing linking the stock drops to the federal government or Dryburgh personally. After consulting his laptop contacts, he slipped out the fourth new phone of the day and dialed the number.

He'd known the guy for a few years, the number of tech geeks, especially those in the higher echelons of corporations, limited to a handful. They had much in common, often sharing the stage at various speaking engagements. Up until this point they'd never collaborated professionally. Layton knew he was going out on a limb, but his options were limited. There weren't many people he trusted in the intelligence business or in the federal government. He suspected that his acquaintance had learned to bridge that gap, although he never advertised it.

It took three rings for the man to pick up. "Neil Patel."

If the president thought the idea of the Russians and their small entourage calling for their U.S. debt was bad, the addition of the Chinese was crippling. As the largest single foreign holder of U.S. debt, China made up approximately eleven percent, or nearly $1.3-trillion, of the stakeholders. Comparatively, Russia owned not even two-percent of U.S. debt. If the Chinese were in bed with the Russians, the U.S. economy would head south quickly.

"Do you really think the Chinese are in play? I know they're communist too, but they hate the Russians," said Zimmer.

"For the most part, they do, but don't forget that either one of them would love to have us out of the way. With one less superpower, they can duke it out in Asia."

"Travis, what do you think?"

The former CEO felt more than out of his league. These men were talking about world domination, and only weeks earlier he'd been worried about his small company in Tennessee. Despite that feeling, he knew wrong from right, and that America should stand as a beacon of hope and prosperity. "I wouldn't put it past the Chinese. We look at things two, maybe five years down the road. These guys are thinking two hundred years into the future. I don't like it one bit, but I think they're just reckless enough to do it."

"So what do we do? Do I need to start throwing threats?" asked the President, the no-win feeling taking hold in the room.

"I think it may still be premature for that, Mr. President," answered Dryburgh.

Zimmer's mood darkened. "Geoff, give me one fucking reason this isn't an act of war."

Dryburgh hesitated. Something about Zimmer's resolve had changed. There was a subtle shift from indecisiveness. He didn't want to push the President too far. He needed him to get there on his own. "Let me get on the phone and start beating the bushes."

The President shook his head. "Not good enough. I want options now."

He'd played right into Dryburgh's hand. The Secretary of State looked uncomfortable for a moment, shifting in his seat, running a hand through his red hair, his gaze on the floor. "It's not much, but I may have one idea."

"Let's hear it."

"I'm not sure how much you'll like it…"

"I said, let's hear it."

Dryburgh resisted the urge to lash out, knowing he had to play the part of humbled servant. "One of my staff heard about some councilman in Connecticut. Apparently the guy came up with a way for us to pay off all our foreign debt in less than six months. I know it sounds crazy…"

"And how does he propose we do that?"

Once again the almost sheepish frown from Dryburgh. "Again, I don't know the particulars, but I think it has something to do with American retirement plans. I over-heard my people laughing about it a couple weeks ago."

"How exactly would that work?" Zimmer's patience was running razor thin.

"I'm not sure, Mr. President. I can have—"

Zimmer pounded the heel of his balled fist on the arm of his seat. "Here's what we're going to do. Put the word out quietly. I want any and all suggestions on how we're going to respond to this threat, including this guy in Connecticut. Fly people in, conference them in if they can't get here in time, but I want all my options on the table by nine o'clock tomorrow morning."

CHAPTER 41

Councilman Jasper Tollis tried not to wake his wife as he snuck into bed, lifting the handmade white and coral patterned quilt his mother-in-law had made them for their wedding twenty years earlier. He hated the thing, and not just because it was pink, but because it reminded him of his lowly station and of his mother-in-law. It seemed like every night he crawled into bed, exhausted, having just spent the entire day fighting for change, but nine times out of ten losing the fight.

Their modest two bedroom home was once owned by the councilman Tollis had beat in his third try, and then only because the ninety-year-old bastard had croaked on the way to the ballot box. Some days Jasper Tollis swore he could hear the old man's ghost walking around the creaky second level, watching and waiting for him in the afterlife.

At first it had been a badge of honor to buy the house for close to nothing, but now it felt like more of a lead weight around his neck, holding him down from ever moving up in life. He was only thirty-seven for Christ's sake! He'd been in office for four years and hadn't made a dent, let alone gotten an offer for any higher office.

He huffed in frustration as he lay back, staring at the popcorn ceiling, yet another project they couldn't afford to do. Just as he closed his eyes, the phone on the bedside table rang. He rushed to stop the clanging of the antique phone, a hand-me-down from Delia's grandparents.

"Hello?"

"Councilman Tollis, please," said a serious voice on the other end of the line.

"This is he."

"Sir, I have the Secretary of State for you."

Tollis went to object, confused, thinking that maybe it was the Secretary of the State of Connecticut, when a familiar voice came through. "Councilman Tollis?"

"Yes…I mean, yes, sir."

"Councilman, I'm calling to inform you that there will be a vehicle coming to get you in less than ten minutes. From your home—"

"Wait, what?" Tollis glanced at his wife, who surprisingly hadn't yet stirred.

"From your home you'll be taken to the airport and flown here."

"Where's here?"

"Washington, D.C. Pack enough for a day or two. I look forward to meeting you in the morning."

The call ended, leaving Jasper Tollis staring at the phone, mouth open, mind whirling.

What the hell was going on?

Similar calls were placed to individuals across the country, the staff of the president's cabinet members doing the legwork, none knowing what it was all about, only that it had all come from the president.

A mix of private charters and military aircraft left locales all bound for the same destination: Washington, D.C.

CHAPTER 42

The White House staff was used to large events, but the last minute notice sent them scrambling. Guests arrived in spurts starting at four in the morning, most looking confused and bleary-eyed. They were ushered in different waiting areas after being told not to talk to one another. Two Secret Service agents stood in each assembly area, ready to pounce on anyone who didn't follow the simple instructions.

President Zimmer was impressed by the showing, and the quick work of his cabinet. But possibly the biggest surprise of all came from the person who'd devised the process by which attendees would arrive, be categorized and presented. After a quick briefing late the night before, it had been Vice President Milton Southgate who volunteered to organize the effort. Zimmer marveled at the precise execution, every member with their marching orders, led by the conductor of the orchestra, Southgate himself.

"Sir, we have twenty of the forty-odd guests already here," reported the Vice President, referring to a printout he had just received from an aide. "As discussed, myself, Mr. Haden, General McMillan and the cabinet members you selected will sort through the proposals. I've allotted no more than fifteen-minutes per. As long as we don't have more than a couple stragglers, that should put us to lunchtime. We'll break for lunch and then reconvene in the Situation Room with you included. I don't think we'll have more than a handful by then, so you can take as long as you'd like to question the guests."

Zimmer was impressed again. The old senator knew what he was doing. He shouldn't be surprised. Southgate knew how to run the show. He was glad he hadn't asked for his resignation. "Thank you for putting this together, Milt. Travis, what do you think?"

Travis nodded his head in agreement. "I've gotta say, Mr. Vice President, you sure as hell know what you're doing."

Southgate nodded. No smile. All business. "By early evening we should have a measure of where we stand. Those with ideas still in the running will be sequestered until I give the word either for them to return home or stay and help with further planning."

"How's morale? Do you think they have any idea why they're here?" asked Zimmer.

Southgate shrugged as if it didn't matter. "All they need to know is that you requested they be here. Apart from that, I've given instructions to keep information to a minimum."

"Good. Let me know how things progress."

The morning went smoothly, thanks to the constant moni-toring of Vice President Southgate. If an attendee, or even a cabinet member, got off topic in even the slightest way, Southgate was there to turn the conversation back to where it needed to be. There had been the young gun from Silicon Valley, obviously full of himself and caffeine, who hadn't taken the hint. After politely asking the man to leave two times, Southgate calmly nodded to the security standing in the recesses of the Situation Room, and the upstart was swiftly escorted away.

By nine o'clock they'd heard a wide variety of concepts. They fell broadly in three categories: military action, rhetoric and economic. Those proposing some kind of military action ranged anywhere from nuclear strikes to assassinating the Russian president. The rhetoric group rode the spectrum anywhere between calling the Russians out on their own economic woes to concocting what really would be called a multi-leveled smear campaign against the Russian government. The economic experts suggested everything from retaliatory tariffs to varying taxation schemes.

By the time they'd adjourned for lunch, Southgate, Travis and the cabinet had whittled the group of forty down to nine.

"So what do you think?" the president asked his Chief of Staff as they each enjoyed a BLT with what must have been half-inch-thick bacon and fried green tomatoes instead of your run-of-the-mill red variety.

"We definitely had some crazies in there. My favorite was the guy who wanted us to send SEALs in to capture the heads of the Russian government and hold them until they said Uncle."

Zimmer chuckled, shaking his head. "I'll bet you would love to be on that mission."

"Sounds good for the movies, but in real life that's just suicide. I'm sure whoever invited that guy felt like an idiot after we grilled him. I mean, the guy didn't even have a way for the SEALs to get out with the hostages. Stupid."

"Well, I did say any and all ideas."

Travis shrugged. "I know, but come on, use your brain, people!"

Zimmer shook his head, smiling. It was good to have Travis in his corner. The former SEAL didn't bow down to him or his office. He gave it to the President from the hip, just like his cousin Cal. "How's the Vice President doing?"

"I can't believe I'm saying this, but Southgate has got his stuff together. I wish you could've seen the cowering after he gave a couple people his death stare. He really puts people in their place."

"Politics and agenda aside, that's why he was so good leading the Senate. My dad used to call him The Iron Fist."

"I see why." Travis placed his plate on the side table and stood up to stretch. "I think we've got a couple good ideas. They may seem out in left field, but given the time constraints and the need for secrecy, I don't see how we could've done much better."

"I can't wait." The President popped the last bite of the BLT in his mouth, knowing that it would probably be the last enjoyable part of his day.

Cal was about to snap. They'd been over the same information time and time again. No leads. No anything.

Martindale had left the night before, but kept in touch throughout the morning.

To make matters worse, Travis called just after midnight, waking Cal with the news of the new Russian threat. They'd batted ideas back and forth, both fearing the worst. The Russians had gotten cocky ever since they'd regained a toe-hold on the world stage. They weren't content with being in anything but first place. Cal had seen firsthand what Russian intelligence agencies were doing in the Middle East. Without much effort to conceal themselves, they casually interacted with countless individuals high on the U.S. target list, terror-ists who were deemed too dangerous to do anything but put a bullet between their eyes or a Tomahawk down their chimney.

Cal rubbed his eyes as he gazed out over the New York City skyline. So many people in such a small area. He wondered what those people would do if they knew what the Russians were planning. If nothing changed, they'd know soon. Would the American people rally together like they had after 9/11? Cal didn't think so. It had taken a coordinated terrorist attack to wake the country, and that only lasted for a short time. Now the United States of America was anything but united. Factions on every side of the table thought they knew how the country should be run. Cal had his own thoughts, and was glad he'd never have to run for office. Keeping his mouth shut was not one of his strong suits.

"Cal, I've got Neil on the phone," said Daniel from across the luxurious room.

Cal turned as the sniper tossed the cell phone to him underhanded. He snatched it out of the air and put it to his ear. "What's up?"

"First, I don't have anything new for you on Martindale's security guy."

Cal groaned. It wasn't like Neil not to produce. "Do you have any good news?"

"Maybe. Have you ever heard of a guy named Jonas Layton?"

"Doesn't ring a bell."

"I'm sure I've mentioned him. We were both at the Ted conference in—"

Cal rolled his eyes. "Neil, can you get to the point?"

"Sorry. Yeah, so this guy Layton is kind of a legend in the tech world. They call him The Fortuneteller."

"Why?"

"The dude it smart." Coming from Neil, that was a huge compliment and Cal knew it. "He's developed a system that enables him to predict future events in a way that's both simple and genius."

"What does he predict?"

"Elections, stock market crashes, economic dips…"

"Wait. Is this the guy who predicted, like, every electoral vote in the last presidential election?"

"Same guy."

"What does this have to do with us?" asked Cal.

"He reached out to me last night. Said he needed help with something."

"And?" Cal loved Neil, the two having been friends for over ten years, but sometimes Neil's lack of situational awareness, namely that Cal was in a very impatient mood, pushed the Marine a bit too far.

"He's working on tracking stocks."

Cal's breath caught. "What did you say?"

"He's pretty sure something's going on with the stock market."

Cal's temper rose. "And why the hell didn't you call me earlier?"

"Take it easy, Cal. Jeez. Sometimes I swear you're gonna bust a blood vessel. Chill out." Neil and Cal both took audible deep breaths. "His initial call was pretty vague. He said he needed help, but didn't know who to turn to. Jonas figured I was a pretty safe bet considering the company I work for. Anyway, we went back and forth over the next few hours. He was pretty jumpy, kept calling from different phone numbers. Finally fessed up to using pay-as-you-go phones he got from a drugstore."

"Why?"

"He says someone might be trying to kill him," said Neil.

"Did he say who?"

"Not yet. Like I said, he's pretty antsy right now. I've offered to help however I can."

"Please tell me this has something to do with what we've been wracking our brains over for the last two days."

"It does. He's tracking the same stocks we are."

CHAPTER 43

Jasper Tollis was exhausted. He glanced around the small waiting room furtively, sipping a cup of ice water as he took in the gold framed pictures of long-dead American leaders. He caught his own scent, a day's worth of nerves and adrenaline having done its duty. What he wouldn't give for a shower, but he didn't dare ask.

As his eyes passed over a delicate vase holding a billowing bunch of lilies, he thought of his wife. The last thing she'd said to him was, "Don't screw it up, Jasper."

She'd always been a bit of a shrew, a trait she picked up from her mother in spades. The constant nagging aside, she'd taken to wearing Jasper's lowly councilman mantel more than he did. She spent his hard-earned dollars at local beauty parlors, telling all the ladies how she was the gem in her husband's eye, his muse.

Nothing could be farther from the truth. He'd loved her once, when they'd met in community college, he a teacher's assistant in both her Econ 101 and Accounting 101 courses, she a sexy little vixen who liked to spend her weekend at the beach. Much to his surprise, she'd taken to him, seeing the determination in his demeanor. She knew he was going somewhere and wanted to be along for the ride. Jasper hadn't thought twice. They'd married and spent every penny of his savings on the small wedding and a week in Tahiti. Things changed as soon as they got home. No more sex. No more school for the new Mrs. Tollis.

After his stint in teaching, Jasper earned two Master's degrees, one in economics and the other in accounting. Looking back he wished his degrees were in law like the majority of his peers. They looked at him like the number-cruncher he was, growing paler by the day in his sunless cubicle.

Jasper Tollis worked hard to get where he was, but an Independent without a clearly defined political party, the Dems too spendy, the Republicans too gun-happy, he was like a sailor without a vessel. He believed he had all the tools to be a successful politician, namely ideas that he thought both practical and innovative, but none of the clout to get there. No patrons paving the way.

To make matters worse, a councilman in a cheap Connecticut district didn't make much money. He had to do his best to take on part-time consulting gigs and accounting freelance work to make ends meet and keep up with his wife's expensive tastes. Maybe the president's summoning could…

Someone's voice shook him from his day-dreaming. "Mr. Tollis?"

Councilman Tollis looked up. "I'm sorry, yes?"

The large agent took pity on the small man who'd become one of the last options standing. "Would you follow me, sir. The president is waiting."

Tollis nodded and got up on shaking legs, almost dumping his files on the floor.

The agent waited patiently. "Sir, if it helps, the President's a pretty good guy. Just be yourself and I'm sure you'll be fine."

Tollis's face turned from a pallid gray to a more solid pink. "Thanks. I think I'm okay now."

He was escorted in to the Situation Room for the second time that day. Many of the same faces from the morning were there, as was President Zimmer. His chaperone pointed to the empty chair across from the President. The men and women sitting around the table went silent and waited for him to find his seat.

Setting his files carefully on the highly polished table, Jasper Tollis gratefully took a seat, his knees still knocking together as he adjusted his chair closer to the conference table.

President Zimmer smiled warmly. "Mr. Tollis, I'd like to thank you for coming on such short notice."

"It's not a problem, Mr. President. Thank you for having me."

The President looked around the room as he spoke. "If no one has any objections, why don't we get down to it. Mr. Tollis, what I am about to tell you doesn't even have a clearance. Let's just say the information and its secrecy are paramount to national security." Zimmer turned to the Vice President and nodded.

Southgate slid a piece of paper across the table to Tollis. "That, Mr. Tollis, is a non-disclosure agreement. By signing it you waive all rights to a fair trial should this information leak to the public through your actions. You will immediately be remanded to custody and stuck in solitary confinement in a federal prison."

Zimmer chuckled, patting Southgate on the arm. "What the Vice President is trying to say is that what we say stays in this room. Got it?"

Jasper Tollis gulped, signing the contract. "Yes, sir."

"Good. Now, early yesterday the Russians contacted us…"

NEW YORK CITY

"How can we meet this guy?" asked Cal.

"I'm not sure he's up for that."

"I don't really care what he's up for, Neil. Tell him we'll guarantee his safety. I can send Gaucho and his team up to get him."

"I'll tell him. Give me a few minutes. I'll call you back."

Cal threw the phone back to Daniel. "Looks like we may have a break in the case, boys."

Councilman Jasper Tollis sat in muted shock. It was hard to believe the Russians were being so brash. Every civilized country in the free world believed in bolstering economic stability, and had lived with a sort of gentleman's truce when it came to the global economy. Sure, the occasional spat over Syria or North Korea was to be expected, but to cast aside a proven investment like American treasury bills was guaranteed catastrophe.

As a long-time student of global economics, Tollis knew, probably better than most of the people in the room what would happen should the Russians, and God forbid the Chinese, call in their U.S. debt.

"So, now that you know the predicament we're in, I'd love to hear about your idea and whether you think it'll help deal with this threat. I will tell you that of the forty or so that came in this morning, nine came back, you being the last. Once I told them the situation, all but five admitted that their ideas were unfeasible. I would appreciate you giving us your honest opinion should you feel the same."

Up until then, Jasper Tollis thought he was one of many economists flown in to help the rising budget tensions in Washington. Not that he thought he had a real shot at the time given the extreme nature of his plan. But now…his mind spun with the possibilities. He'd been laughed at and cast aside for what many had called a stupid proposition. Even his wife said the solution was 'half-baked.' If those idiots in Connecticut could only see him now.

After regaining his composure, Tollis sat up a bit straighter and looked the President in the eye for the first time. "Mr. President, I think my plan will work."

CHAPTER 44

Jasper Tollis took a sip of water from the glass sitting on the table in front of him. The room was deathly quiet, all eyes on him. He was surprised at the lack of smell in the room, probably some futuristic air filtration system that kept the body odors of adrenaline-fueled politicians at bay during times of crisis.

He felt once again in command of his body. He had center stage.

"Mr. President, as I'm sure you already know, the current national debt stands at around twenty-three trillion dollars. A majority of that, despite what the media would have you believe, is held by everyday Americans, American municipalities, brokerages and our own federal government through things like Social Security and the Federal Reserve. The total percentage of that twenty-three trillion owned by foreign entities currently stands at thirty-four percent. The largest portions go to China, then Japan. If what you say is true about China, Russia and some of the other larger stakeholders, we could see a dramatic hit to not only our stock markets, but those around the world."

"How do you propose we deal with it?"

Tollis smiled, ready for the coming rebuttals from the room. "My plan is simple. Tax all U.S. retirement accounts at ninety-percent and pay off the entire twenty-three-trillion-dollar bill in one fell swoop."

The room was silent as the President digested the news, his face showing no signs of confusion or distaste. "What accounts would this affect?"

"Retirement accounts like the 401-k, IRAs, you name it."

"Don't you think the American people might be a little pissed that we're taking all their money?" asked Zimmer.

Tollis didn't search to see who the chuckle from the end came from. "At first they will be, Mr. President, but this has to be sold as a plan for the greater good, an opportunity to be out of the hands of the Chinese and Russians. I've also devised a way that the federal government can re-release treasury bills and bonds at reduced rates, but with increased returns. That way we're incentivizing our citizens to invest at home instead of abroad."

"And what about the countries like Japan that don't want to see us go belly up?"

"They'll have to deal with it. However, now that you've brought the Japanese up, Mr. President, did you know that Japan's debt is by and large owned by its own people? For years the media has talked about the debt Japan owes, but it owes it to the Japanese."

Zimmer nodded. "So you're saying we take a page out of the Japanese playbook."

"To a certain degree, Mr. President. The Japanese are still over-leveraged. With all our resources, we don't have to be that way. Japan imports everything they need. We're a major exporter, even now with oil and the boom happening in the Dakotas. Hell, Mr. President, we could become a self-sustained superpower the likes the world has never seen."

Jasper Tollis was breathing heavily, having excited himself into a near frenzy. Just the fact that the President was listening at all made his plan real. For the first time since he'd come up with the idea, Jasper Tollis truly believed it could work.

"Well, Mr. Tollis, you sure have given us something to think about."

———

Once their guest had been escorted from the Situation Room, those assembled exploded into conversation, most directed at the President.

"I think we should go with the first option, Mr. President."

"We need military action, Mr. President."

"Let's widen the search, Mr. President."

Zimmer sat back and listened to the ruckus, still digesting everything he'd heard. It was Vice President Southgate who stood, rapping his ashen knuckles on the solid table. "Gentlemen, why don't we take an hour break for dinner and then reconvene at seven."

The President stood, prompting the rest of the room to follow suit. "Sounds good to me. I'm starved."

———

President Zimmer invited Travis Haden, Secretary of State Dryburgh, General McMillan and Vice President Southgate to join him for dinner in the Oval Office. He wanted to come up with a game plan before heading back downstairs. His national security advisor would have joined them, but he'd gotten an urgent call as they'd adjourned.

The space felt electrified to Zimmer. The air buzzed with anticipation, energy focused toward a single purpose. He'd started the day unsure of where it would lead, but the past few hours had shown him that there could be a way out, a solution to deal with the Russians and their allies. Now he was famished once again, devouring the bacon cheeseburger and fries in front of him before saying a word.

The others chatted quietly while they ate, not wanting to intrude on the President's thoughts. Zimmer balled up his paper napkin and landed a perfect free throw into the waste basket.

"Well, gentlemen, what are your thoughts?" He turned to Gen. McMillan first, curious to see which way the chairman of the Joint Chiefs was leaning.

"Mr. President, frankly I think a flat-out *hell no* might do the trick. I don't see how military action would achieve much of anything other than to escalate tensions. I think you're already doing the right thing in preparing to take a strong stance against this."

"I won't lie, General, I'm actually happy to hear you say that. I wasn't sure what you'd say."

McMillan smiled, his bulldog wrinkles forming concave arcs at the sides of his mouth. "I may be a Marine, Mr. President, but I'm not a war monger. Sometimes a few words can be more powerful than the Seventh Fleet floating into town."

Zimmer nodded, knowing that McMillan had a deep grasp of history, and was in the process of writing his third book. He'd have to ask the Marine how he ever found the time.

"Geoff, what do you think?"

All eyes turned to Dryburgh, who'd been quiet throughout the day. He still looked a bit jet-lagged from the day before, gray circles under his eyes and his red hair not as polished as it usually was. "As I've said before, Mr. President, a strong stance is needed. Unlike the general, however, I'm not sure we should take any of our options off table quite yet. We all know the Russians don't listen to much, but they sure as hell listen to force. Reagan showed them that in the eighties."

"Travis, what about you?"

Travis shook his head with a laugh. "If you told me six months ago that this is what we'd be dealing with, I would've thought you were crazy. That being said, and I know you may think *I'm* crazy, but this idea from the councilman from Connecticut is growing on me."

That surprised the President. He knew that Travis Haden, former SEAL and CEO of an international security and R&D firm, was a staunch conservative. It was one of the reasons he'd wanted him as his Chief of Staff, to play devil's advocate to the president's left-leaning tendencies.

"Why the change?"

"I'll say that I agree with both the secretary and the general. We need to be firm, that's a given. But this may be our chance to get out of this whole debt mess. I've always hated the idea that America is beholden to anyone. I know it's supposed to be a way of life now, but it just aggravates the hell out of me. If we can come up with a way to convince the American people that it's not only a way out of the Russian fiasco, but also an end to our financial woes, hell it might be worth a shot."

Everyone in the room took a moment to digest Travis's declaration, obviously a surprise by the looks on everyone's faces.

Vice President Southgate took a measured sip of his tea and said, "First, let me say that I agree with Mr. Haden. We've given away too much power, to China especially, and I fear that if we go at the same pace, they, and others, may one day have all the incentive they need to take over control of our country. Second, although I agree with the recommendation, I'm not sure we're ready for it. Do not doubt that the reaction will be swift and furious. Americans will beat down our doors and call us thieves in the night. That's one problem. The second, one I believe more detrimental, is the fact that we as politicians do a poor job managing the money we're given." Southgate looked across at Travis. "Yes, Mr. Haden, I know you may be shocked to hear me say that, but I've been in Washington long enough to know that government may not be the best solution to all of America's woes. That being said, I still think we should take a hard look at Mr. Tollis's proposal."

It was like Southgate had admitted to being a woman. Zimmer found it hard not to stare at the old senator. To those in the know, it was fairly common knowledge that politicians spent money faster than a gambling addict in Vegas, but to say it out loud, and by a veteran former-senator no less, was quite the revelation.

Travis coughed to keep from laughing. Gen. McMillan rubbed his hands together. Secretary of State Dryburgh stared out the window. President Zimmer took it all in, the recommendations sound, but not quite what he'd expected. It didn't matter. He felt different than he had for months. Whether it was the fact that an insidious drug no longer coursed through his veins or that he'd come to grips with his new position, President Brandon Zimmer would not sit by and watch a foreign power bully his beloved country.

"Okay, gentlemen, let's come up with a plan."

CHAPTER 45

It was determined that they should adjourn until morning. They still had time to decide, and would reconvene at 6:00 a.m. Vice President Southgate volunteered to deliver the news to the rest of the cabinet. Dryburgh and McMillan both said their goodbyes and left, each heading back to their respective offices.

That left the President alone in the Oval Office with Travis. After the excitement of the day, they were happy to take a much-needed load off. Zimmer loosened his tie while Travis took off his navy blue suit jacket and tossed it onto the back of the couch. He looked to his boss. "Would you think less of me if I ordered a glass of bourbon?"

"Only if you don't get one for me."

They waited for their drinks to arrive, purposefully talking about things other than business, knowing that they'd have another long day ahead of them. Round and round was the game of politics played.

After a couple healthy swigs from their bourbons, they turned back to the task at hand.

"How about Southgate coming out of left field?" asked Travis. "My eyes almost popped out of my head."

"It may still be too early to say this, but I think Southgate's coming around. Fingers crossed that he's seen the error of his ways, and God willing, understands that he is not infallible."

"I would not have believed it in a million years. You really pulled a rabbit out of your hat when you asked him to be your number two. Shit, I thought you were crazy."

Zimmer laughed. "Maybe I was!"

Travis almost spit out the drink in his mouth. "Jesus."

Zimmer laughed louder as Travis tried not to let the burning liquid come out of his nose, pinching it with two fingers. "You okay?"

Travis nodded, wincing. "Damn. You got me there." He shook his head, clearing the pain, and then took another careful sip. "You have an idea of where you want to take this whole Russia thing?"

Zimmer did. His mind had conceived an option during the hours of listening to his advisors and their guests. It was so clear. He wondered if that's what had happened to Kennedy during the Cuban missile crisis, or Reagan during the Iran-Contra affair.

"I think so."

The look on Zimmer's face made Travis cock his head. "You look like you've got your mind made up. What is it?"

"Let me sleep on it, possibly with the help of one more of these." The president lifted up his empty cocktail and nodded for another.

Dryburgh stomped into his office, ignoring the call from his secretary who asked if he needed anything before she left for the day. Closing his door behind him, he flung his winter coat across the room, pumping his arm in exultation. He was so close. The President was bending just the way he wanted. He could've kissed Haden for what he'd said over dinner. Dryburgh had planned on the former CEO being one of his biggest hurdles.

On the other hand, in his excitement he'd wanted to reach over for the Vice President's neck and strangle him. He would've thought the classic liberal to be 100% on-board for taxing the American people. Something had changed with Southgate. He was still the ornery old eccentric, but now he looked almost like a team player, a fact that completely baffled Dryburgh. Not a week earlier it had been Southgate who'd given him the information on the President's collusion with Haden and his associates. He had no idea what had changed, but it didn't sit well with the bold Secretary of State. He hadn't risen as far as he had without knowing everything about his friends and enemies alike.

But he didn't think it would matter. He had the president's attention. With that, along with the help of a few outside forces, he wouldn't have to do a thing. President Zimmer would bring about his own undoing, leaving one man in the perfect position to take over the presidency: Geoffrey Dryburgh.

—◆—

Congressman McKnight didn't like the silence. He'd always equated the lack of noise to some impending doom. As a child it was his father's return from another rathole, reeking of cheap whiskey, staggering in, demanding this and that from his wife, inevitably ending with a thorough beating.

So as he sat in his office, the last one there, with no noise, not even his usually buzzing phone, his mind started to wander, his heartbeat ticking faster. He stood up suddenly, nearly knocking over the glass of water on his paper-scattered desk. Grabbing it just in time, saving the paperwork he'd finally gotten from the Secret Service concerning the untimely death of Santos Lockwood. They'd determined the cause of death to be a massive heart attack. Instant death. *Damn him.*

Without Lockwood's updates, he was effectively blind to the goings-on at the White House. The good news was that not a word had been said to him about his involvement. They had, however, made the connection with the Russian scientist. McKnight imagined it was only a matter of time before the black market capitalist was nabbed by a few commandos and whisked to an undisclosed location for interrogation.

With his involvement not even on the radar, McKnight could focus on just how he wanted to exploit the President's weaknesses. Until he could get another mole inside the White House, it wouldn't be a bad idea to back off and regroup. Besides, he had Santos's mother to deal with. Maybe he could somehow convince the Secret Service to expedite transporting Lockwood's remains home. Until then, he was stuck consoling the grieving widow. Six phones calls that day. He couldn't take much more of it. His capacity for empathy was waning quickly.

He had to get back to the task at hand, namely how to further discredit the President, and by doing so, any other contenders in the Democratic Party. The American people had to first come to the conclusion that their votes must lean right. It was already happening in congressional districts across the country. The next logical step was the White House.

Even though the presidential primaries were still years away, there were steps to take, donors to align, plans to be made. In some circles he was becoming a contender. The voice of the new Republican Party. That's what they were calling him. There was much to do, but McKnight had faith in his abilities. In three years it would be him sitting in the Oval Office, commanding the attention of the world, and finally showing his father that he could be somebody.

CHAPTER 46

Travis nodded to the agent outside the door, and entered the Oval Office. The lights were dimmed and the fire wasn't lit. For a moment he wasn't sure if the President was even there until the chair behind the large desk swiveled around.

President Zimmer was already dressed in what he'd told Travis was his 'presidential' attire, a navy suit, robin's egg shirt and a blood red tie patterned with tiny impressions of George Washington, impossible to pick up unless you looked very closely.

"You look like you're ready to go on television," Travis joked, making his way to one of the chairs on the opposite side of the President's desk.

"I am," said Zimmer, not a hint of play in his countenance, unwaveringly determined.

Travis glanced at his watch in confusion. "I'm sorry, did I forget about something? I thought—"

"Change of plans. I'm going on at six thirty."

A feeling of dread crept into Travis's stomach. He didn't sit down. "What's the occasion?"

There was something in Zimmer's eyes that reminded Travis of one of his SEAL instructors, a command master chief everyone called Old Smokey. The man constantly puffed on a cigar or had it jammed in the corner of his mouth. He had a way of glaring at you that made you believe he would have his way, no matter the price.

"I thought a lot about this whole debacle last night and I realized the answer was sitting right in front of me, plain as day."

"Would you like to tell me what that is?" The unease subsided somewhat, Travis getting a feel for his boss's vibe. It was like a commander who suddenly saw the weakness in the enemy's defenses. Exploit it.

Zimmer chuckled, his eyes still cold. "I took for granted the power of this office. I was so worried about not making waves that I forgot what my job was. That ends today."

"And you're going to do that by..."

This time there was a genuine smile on the President's face. It drew Travis in and even made him take a seat, wanting, no, needing to know where Zimmer was heading.

"I learned it from you and Cal. Overwhelming force, right?"

Travis nodded, still not understanding.

"You said yourself the only thing the Russians and the Chinese respect is force. Well, I'm about to give them some."

NATIONAL BURDEN

Paul Dowse was a first year reporter with the *Washington Times*. He'd been pulling an all-nighter when his boss called from home ordering him to The White House. Paul had luckily been one of the first to arrive, snagging a seat in the second row, the first being saved for the craggy veteran reporters who always seemed to get their questions answered. He'd never been to a White House briefing, so everything felt alive despite the bored looks on the faces of the tired camera crews and the other reporters straggling in. No one knew what the President was going to say, but that didn't mean it was going to be big news. Zimmer could just be using the early time slot as practice for the future. He'd been shy with the media up until that point.

The news conference was so last minute that only half of the normal press corps were present as the President took the stage, grim as he walked up to the podium. Behind him streamed his new Chief of Staff, the Vice President, Secretary of State Dryburgh and Gen. McMillan. Paul leaned over and nudged the reporter next to him, a balding guy with coffee breath and hair coming out of his ear.

"You know what this is about?"

The man looked at him like he was an idiot. "No."

Paul wanted to tell the man to chill the fuck out, but the President began.

"Fellow Americans, I come before you today with news of another threat to our national security."

The room perked up, all eyes now focused on the podium.

"Two days ago, we received word from our friends in Russia. I use the term friends loosely in this case."

Paul started scribbling in his notepad, wanting to get the best tidbits, a feeling that this was to be a momentous speech.

"The communication was brief, but firm. Despite our years of friendship and untold billions of aid, Russia has now decided to cash in, to call all the U.S. debt it holds. Not only that, they have also convinced certain other countries, who will for now remain nameless, to do the same."

The air left the room. Reporters leaned forward, some with recorders outstretched, wanting to capture every word.

"Russia has given us the ultimatum to pay back the investments they made in good faith, and that we provided in kind, in seventy-two hours." Zimmer looked directly in the main camera, his eyes burning, more determined than the young reporter had ever seen him. "While this may come as a shock to most of you, it is, in fact, within Russia's right to cash in its chips, to step away from the table."

Zimmer smiled, still staring at the camera. "Fellow Americans, I've come to you with a solution, a way to reconsolidate all federal debt back to the United States, so that we will no longer be bullied by our supposed friends across the sea. As soon as I leave this room, and with the help of the Vice President and the Cabinet, I will be sending an emergency bill to the House floor. The summarized details will be released to media outlets and posted on The White House website within the hour. The American Investment Initiative will be voted on before the close of business today. If your elected officials cannot come to a consensus, I will institute my plan through the executive powers given to me by the Constitution of the United States. I hope it will not come to that. Now, this may not seem like the best deal for you, but trust me when I say that in the long run, it will make us stronger and less dependent on foreign money. If the international community no longer feels we are a good investment, we will take that investment back. Desperate times call for desperate measures, and this is one of those times. But out of this ordeal shines brilliant opportunity. An economic opportunity we have not had in over one-hundred years. We will once again show the world that we value our friendships, but that we will not be bullied."

Travis caught up to the President as he left the shouting reporters in the briefing room. It was like he'd said they'd just had another 9/11 or dropped an atomic bomb on Nagasaki. Utter chaos as the President's men filed out behind him.

"You sure that was the best idea?" Travis whispered to the President. He'd known the gist of what Zimmer was going to say, but hearing it said out loud had taken every ounce of self-control he had not to show surprise.

Zimmer nodded, walking purposefully down the hallway. "Just wait. I'm sure the phone calls will be coming in now."

The President was right. Ellen was in a frenzy when they neared the Oval Office. She looked up, flashing lights blinking up and down on the two phones on her desk. "Mr. President, I…"

President Zimmer walked over to the faithful public servant and placed a hand on her shoulder. "Take a deep breath, Ellen."

"But all these calls, I don't know—"

"Tell them all that I'm unavailable and will return their calls as soon as I can." He smiled at her reassuringly. She tried her best to nod, but instead turned back to the blinking wrath.

Travis felt sorry for her. It was going to be a long day for the White House staff.

By 7 a.m. every major stock exchange in the world was closed. By 7:15 a.m., almost every world leader was in a closed meeting with their closest advisors.

The Russians were in a state of shock. Troops had to be called into Moscow to close down main thoroughfares. Thousands were making their way to the capital on foot as the Kremlin braced itself.

In one fell swoop, President Zimmer had exposed Russia's plan and enraged the rest of the world to such a level that presidents, prime ministers, bankers, CEOs and world citizens were all looking to Russia for an explanation. As was their way, instead of responding immediately, Russia closed its gates, letting the mobs grow, becoming more mobilized by the minute.

By 7:30 a.m. the entire world had heard the details of Zimmer's plan. The American government would tax all U.S. retirement plans at ninety-percent, giving them more than enough cash to recall all forms of investment, not only held in foreign hands, but also held within the United States. The next step would be to reissue higher interest bonds and treasury bills only to Americans, at a reduced rate, of course.

There was no telling how long markets would be shuttered. The impact of the news had been deafening, like a thousand explosions going off all over the world.

Through it all, President Zimmer stayed in the Oval Office, monitoring the news with his Chief of Staff and Vice President Southgate. Few words were said, and no advice was given. His men knew America's card had been played and that it would only be a matter of time before they got an answer.

CHAPTER 47

The helicopter landed softly on the rooftop pad, kicking up swirls of snow in the process and making Cal, Daniel and Trent shield their eyes. They hadn't waited long, the pilot making good time despite the airspace traffic.

The side hatch eased open, the passenger careful not to let the draft slam it forward. After leaning over to say something to the pilot, the man closed the door and made his way to the waiting three.

Cal stuck out his hand as the helicopter pilot applied power and lifted the bird back into the sky, away in seconds.

"Mr. Layton, I'm Cal Stokes. These are my associates, Daniel Briggs and Willy Trent."

Jonas Layton shook Cal's hand. "Please, call me Jonas."

Cal nodded. "How about we head over to the hotel."

"Sounds good to me. I've had my fill of heights for the day."

They'd talked briefly over the phone, Cal finally convincing the cautious Layton to meet him in New York. It was plain to see the man was on edge, his eyes darting as they drove the five blocks back to the Peninsula. Cal kept the conversation light, MSgt Trent providing the comic relief. Daniel drove in silence, alert as usual.

Once they'd stepped back into their palatial suite, Daniel taking Layton's coat, they got down to business. Cal dove right in.

"Tell us about what happened in Paris."

Layton told them about the attempted kidnapping, impressing Cal with his level of detail and detachment. Most non-military citizens froze or ran in life or death events. Layton then described who had helped him.

"It's a good thing you knew that French guy," said Cal.

"I've made it my business to foster a lot of mutually beneficial relationships over the years. I like to think my friends far outweigh my enemies."

Cal didn't say what he was thinking, that you could have all the friends in the world, but it only took one enemy to make your life miserable, or worse, end it.

"Neil told us what you do, and we've done a little research online, but I'm still confused. How did you get involved in this?"

Layton looked uncomfortable, pinching the bridge of his nose. "That's a complicated question."

"Why don't you start at the beginning?"

Again, Layton paused before answering. "I don't know how comfortable I am telling you. The people that are after me…"

"Look. We do this for a living, Jonas. We've all been shot at more times than we can count. We don't scare easily. Why don't you just tell us?"

"I just have a feeling this goes much higher than you guys could imagine."

"Let me guess, you think someone in the government is involved."

Layton nodded. "I'm not sure yet, but it may have implications up to the president."

Cal felt a jolt pass through his body. "Wait. What are you talking about?"

"I can't prove it yet, but I think the current administration may be behind this whole thing."

The White House staff was on high alert, running to and fro with phones glued to their ears or eyes fixed on tablets. So many calls were coming in that they'd had to stop answering the anonymous ones and solely focus on those they knew, or thought they knew, were important. Ellen Hanson, the President's secretary, played gatekeeper almost as much as the augmented security staff. She had piles of messages for the President.

But the President didn't want to be bothered; he hadn't returned one phone call. Instead, he sat calmly in the Oval Office, watching the storm like a disinterested outsider, quickly glancing at each new message, sometimes frowning, sometimes with an amused look on his face.

Ellen couldn't fathom what her boss was doing. Shouldn't he be trying to fix the mess he'd made? Shouldn't he have the courtesy to return at least a handful of the calls?

But that wasn't her job. She did what she could, sifting through the growing weeds, sorting as she went. As the morning wore on, her mind quietly analyzed the situation, the determined look of the President, the way he kept saying, "It's going to be fine, Ellen."

Truth be told, she hadn't known what to think of the President for months. He'd seemed nice enough, but somehow, not up to snuff. Now it was different. There was a certain air of confidence he hadn't had in weeks past. This was a new man, a leader.

Ellen smiled at the thought, then pursed her lips and got back to the task at hand.

———

"I assume you've seen what's happening in Washington right now?" asked Cal.

"Of course. But I think the President's speech has something to do with this."

Cal almost laughed at Layton's comment. How could the man they called The Fortuneteller be so wrong? Cal knew Zimmer, knew why he'd done what he had. How could Layton possibly think the President somehow had a hand in orchestrating the Russian offensive? "Look, I'm not sure how much you know about the President, but he happens to be—"

Cal's phone buzzed on the table, everyone looking down as the caller ID popped up: Neil Patel. "Let me get that."

Cal picked up the phone and stood. "What's up?"

"Hey, are you watching the news?"

"It's on mute."

"Oh, okay. Hey, I've got something for you. I was finally able to find something that may be of value. You told me to track down the security chief's movement over the past month. Well, Martindale's head of security got a safety deposit box two weeks before he was murdered. It's about a mile from where you're staying. I'm not sure it'll help, but it's something."

"You think you can get me access?"

"Of course."

"Okay. Send me the information. I feel worthless here. We'll head out now."

Cal ended the call and looked to his friends. "Well, fellas, looks like we don't have to sit on our asses for the next hour. Let's go rob a bank."

Ellen opened the door to the Oval Office cautiously, her heart thrumming, excited energy coursing through her fifty-year-old body. The President was still behind his desk, flipping through the last batch of messages she'd brought in minutes earlier. He looked up. "More messages?"

Ellen glanced at Mr. Haden and the Vice President. "Um, no, sir."

Zimmer motioned her over, a warm smile to embolden her steps. She walked around the desk and handed him the blue sticky note, almost not letting go. Zimmer grabbed the note and read it, one eyebrow rising as a smile tugged at the corner of his mouth. "Thank you, Ellen. I trust you'll keep this to yourself?"

"Of course, Mr. President."

Ellen Hanson turned and headed for the door, realizing suddenly that she'd just witnessed history being made. Even if she could tell her husband, he'd never believe her.

CHAPTER 48

President Zimmer read the note again, shaking his head. Travis and Southgate looked on, waiting to hear what it said.

"Looks like we've got a live one, gentlemen."

"Who is it?" asked Travis.

Zimmer held up a finger and picked up the desktop phone, referencing the sticky note and dialing a number. He waited for the pickup. "Yes, I got your message."

Silence as the President nodded and listened to the other end.

"Yes, give me the address and I'll have my people pick you up."

Zimmer flipped the sticky note over and wrote something on the other side. "Got it. Yes, thank you. I look forward to seeing you."

He hung up the phone and looked up at Travis. "Can you see if Brett's outside?"

Travis nodded and walked to the door and opened it. He said something to the agent standing post and the man spoke into his lapel mic.

Two minutes later, Brett Stayer, the head of Zimmer's security detail, marched in. "Yes, Mr. President?"

Zimmer waved the sticky note in the air and said, "There's an address on here. I want you to send a small team, discreetly, to go pick up the person at this house and bring him here. Oh, and if you could bring him in the back way, that would probably be best. I don't want anyone else seeing him."

Stayer walked over and grabbed the note. "Yes, sir. I'll take them myself."

"That would be best. Thank you, Brett."

"Yes, sir."

Stayer left and Travis spoke up first. "Now can you tell us what's going on?"

Zimmer rubbed his hands together. "Things are about to get interesting."

NEW YORK CITY

Daniel let Cal off at the curb. He and Trent would swing back around when Cal was finished, or arrested. As they pulled back into traffic, Cal looked up at the door. It didn't look like a bank. It looked more like a high end shoe store. He couldn't see any teller counters inside, just modern desks with professionally, if not elegantly, attired workers.

He stepped in the door, the subtle smell of pomegranate and some flower he couldn't place greeting him along with the long-legged blonde who stepped out from around her desk as soon as the door chimed.

"Good morning, sir. How may I help you?"

Having already hacked into the bank's system, it was easy for Neil to replace the true owner's pictures with one of Cal's head shots. Luckily the state's government services had yet to report the man's death to the financial institution. The signature samples were also substituted with Cal's handwriting. A paper copy of the deceased driver's ID was now graced by Cal's likeness thanks to Neil's DMV back end intrusion, and he had all the codes needed for entrance. The customer service oriented bank manager happily gave Cal access to the deposit box.

Ten minutes later, Cal was saying his goodbyes and thank you's, the twenty-some teller going so far as to give him her card should he need further assistance. He smiled and departed.

Daniel found a spot across the congested pavement and double-tapped the horn to get Cal's attention. He caught his friend's eye with a wave, and Cal headed over.

Once he was safely in the passenger seat, Daniel pulled out into traffic and headed toward the hotel.

"What did you get?" asked Daniel.

Cal stuck his hand in his pants pocket and held up a thumb drive with the Dale & Moon logo on it, a moon superimposed over a meadow. "This was it. I guess we'll see when we get back."

NATIONAL BURDEN

Zimmer had instructed his security to not allow anyone to enter the Oval Office until he gave the word. Roughly thirty minutes after departing, Brett Stayer opened the side door and ushered the President's guest in.

The President rose and walked to greet him. "Mr. Ambassador, how nice to see you again."

Igor Bukov, the Russian Ambassador to the United States, had a fedora pulled low in an obvious attempt to conceal his face. He pulled it off and shook the President's hand, a hand that Zimmer noticed trembled as he took it. "Thank you, Mr. President." Zimmer could smell the vodka on the man's breath.

"Why don't we have a seat. Could I get you anything?" asked Zimmer.

Bukov glanced nervously at Travis and the Vice President, and said with a touch of embarrassment, "A glass of vodka would be very much appreciated, Mr. President."

"Done."

As Travis placed the order, the Russian took a seat in the chair closest to the fire, as if he needed the added warmth. He did not take off his overcoat, but rather just stared into the flames somberly.

Once he'd settled into his own chair, the president said, "Mr. Ambassador, why don't you tell the Vice President and Mr. Haden what you asked me over the phone."

Bukov nodded, not looking up from the fire. Then, as if it took every ounce of strength he had left, he sighed and turned back to the others. "Mr. President, gentlemen, I am here to officially request asylum in your country."

———•———

Jonas Layton was talking with Neil on a video conference when the others returned to their hotel suite. He had head-phones in his ears and didn't even notice them when they walked in. *Situational awareness, dude*, thought Cal. He tapped Layton on shoulder, making him jump.

"Oh, hey."

Cal waved and held up the thumb drive to Neil on the computer screen. "Got something."

Neil squinted. "Have you tried to access it yet?"

"Nope. Thought you and Jonas might be better at that."

"Jonas, do you mind if Cal uses your computer?" asked Neil.

"Go for it."

Cal handed the thumb drive to Jonas, who removed the cap and inserted it into his laptop. The three Marines looked over his shoulder as he attempted to access the files. "Looks like it's encrypted." Jonas clicked a button to share the screen-shot with Neil. "Neil, you seeing this?"

"Yeah. Be careful. It looks like it may have some kind of kill switch."

Jonas did a bunch of clicking and dragging that Cal only half understood. He knew enough about computers, but was nowhere near the level of Jonas and Neil.

"I think I've got it." With one more click, the sole folder opened, now showing others. "Where should I start?"

"Click on the one that says SVID," suggested Cal.

Jonas did. When it opened there were maybe twenty files labeled numerically. "Want me to play one?"

"Yes," said Cal.

Jonas double-clicked on the first file and a new screen popped up, taking a moment to load the video. When it finally did, the five men watched as a grid of four surveillance videos came up. They watched for a couple minutes, no one saying a thing, trying to capture the significance.

"This could take forever," said Trent, already bored by the display.

"Why don't we try one of the other folders," said Cal.

Once again, Jonas did as instructed, double-clicking on another folder and opening the first file inside. This one contained some type of ledger, or was it a bank statement? Cal couldn't tell.

"Tell you what. Jonas, could you send this over to Neil so his guys can dissect it?" asked Cal.

"No problem. Sending it now, Neil."

"Cool. I'll let you know when I've got something," said Neil, already diving in.

Neil's face disappeared and Jonas shut the laptop.

Cal took a seat, and leveled his gaze onto Jonas. "Let's get back to the conversation we were having before we left. I'm curious to know why you think the President could be involved with the Russians."

Jonas's mouth became a hard line. Cal could tell he didn't want to say. Did that mean he was involved, too? He was going to kill Neil if that was the case.

Jonas exhaled and returned Cal's stare. "It was Geoffrey Dryburgh who tried to have me kidnapped."

CHAPTER 49

It was like time had stopped in the Oval Office. President Zimmer looked to Travis then to Vice President Southgate. Both men speechless.

"My God," whispered the President.

Ambassador Bukov had explained the rationale behind the incursion in Lithuania and the coalition to tank the dollar. Behind it all had been one man, Geoffrey Dryburgh.

"Mr. President, I must say that I am ashamed of my role in this charade."

"You sure as hell wouldn't have felt sorry if you'd gotten away with it," snapped Travis.

Bukov didn't disagree. "What can I say? It is part of the game we play."

Zimmer interjected before Travis could say anything. "What was the end goal? Why would Dryburgh want us to look bad? Surely he knew it would come back on him as well."

The Russian shrugged. "He did not tell me this, but I believe he had planned on using either scenario to see you removed from office. Lithuania might not have done it, but at the time your support within your country was not as strong as it could have been. Now, with the debt crisis, I believe he somehow would have helped public sentiment turn against you. Not that it would be hard. Again, this is merely speculation on my part."

Zimmer knew the second part was especially true. He'd known it would be a gamble taking money from Americans, but it had seemed like the only shot.

"How did you come to the conclusion that asylum was your only course?"

Bukov laughed. He was in a better mood than when he'd arrived, already having downed three glasses of vodka and now feeling safe within the confines of the American capital. "The leaders of my country are not as forgiving as you, Mr. President. I was able to convince them that the Lithuania ploy had not been my fault, although I'm ashamed to say one of my underlings disappeared after the fact. But the idea to play off of your national debt was my idea, at least in their minds. Early this morning I got word from a friend that a team of assassins was on their way to find me. Luckily I'd had my television on when you gave your speech or I might not be here now."

It was so crazy that Zimmer almost didn't believe it. How could Dryburgh be so reckless, so stupid? Maybe there was a chance that Bukov was lying just to save his own skin.

Before he could ask more about Bukov's relationship with Dryburgh, Travis interrupted. "Sir, I just got a text from Cal. He says he needs to talk to you now."

"Can't it wait?"

"He said 911, sir. He never says that."

"Dial his number and give me the phone."

Travis speed dialed his cousin and handed the cell phone to the President. Zimmer ignored the confused look on the face of the soon-to-be-drunk Bukov.

"Cal, it's Brandon."

"Oh, hey."

"What's up? We're kind of in the middle of something right now."

"Yeah, sorry. I just thought that you should know. We've got proof that Dryburgh is in on the debt deal with the Russians."

"Wait, what? How did you get it?"

"It's a long story, but we've got him. He's been testing the market, muscling his way into companies...I can explain later, but I just thought you should know."

Zimmer couldn't find the words to reply for a moment.

"You still there, Brandon?"

"Yeah. Thanks for the heads-up."

"No problem. How are you doing?"

"I'm...I'll be okay." Zimmer shook the cobwebs of shock from his mind. "Hey, how quick can you get down here?"

"We're still wrapping things up in New York, but..."

"I need you here now."

"No problem. I'll let you know when we land."

President Zimmer handed the phone back to Travis and looked to Ambassador Bukov. "Ambassador, I'm happy to grant you asylum in our country, but there's a favor I'll be needing first."

Cal pocketed his phone and moved to grab his gear. "Change of plans. We're all going to D.C."

Daniel and MSgt Trent nodded. It was Jonas who looked up in surprise. "Me too?"

"Unless you wanna sit here by yourself, I think it might be good idea." Cal could tell by the look on Jonas's face that he wanted to go anywhere but the nation's capital.

Trent walked over to the wizard billionaire and offered him a hand up from his seat. "Don't worry, Jonas. I won't leave your side."

Whether it was the thought of being alone, or the comfort of having the near seven foot power of MSgt Willy Trent as his protector, Jonas Layton gathered his belongings and prepared to leave with the others.

As they went to board the private elevator, Cal's phone buzzed in his pocket. He took it out and glanced at the text. His eyes went wide. "No fucking way."

"What is it?" asked Daniel.

Cal shook his head, eyes steeled. "We've gotta make one stop before we head south."

———◆———

They pulled into the stone drive, the large black gates opening with a yawn, fog hanging lazily on the perfectly trimmed grass. Daniel drove the rented sedan around the curving path and up to their destination. The sprawling mansion awaited, Leo Martindale standing inside the front glass door. He was talking to someone, and it took Cal a moment to realize Leo was on the phone with a bluetooth in his ear. He waved to Cal as he got out of the car. Cal bent down to talk to his companions.

"Top, you stay here with Jonas. Daniel, why don't you come with me. I may need your help remembering some of the details."

Daniel left the car running and stepped out into the cool Southampton air. Cal led the way in, the front door already held open by Leo. He pointed to his ear indicating that he was still on the phone. Cal nodded.

They followed the billionaire through the house as Leo finished his call. When they got to the kitchen, he pulled out his earpiece and set it on the reclaimed wood countertop.

"What going on? Did you guys find something?" asked Leo, grabbing a Smart Water from the fridge.

"We did," answered Cal.

"So?"

Cal put a finger to his lips and pointed up as if to say someone was listening.

"I'm the only one here. My family's tucked away in Vail until this thing blows over and I had the staff leave so I could have some privacy."

"Let's talk out back," Cal suggested.

Leo's eyes scrunched in confusion, but he nodded. "Let me just grab my coat."

"Tell me where it is and I'll catch up with you," said Daniel.

"We're tight on time, Leo. We've got a flight out in less than an hour," said Cal, already headed to the backyard.

Again, the confused look. "Okay. My coat's in the front closet next to the door we came in through. Grab the one with EGA on the front, will you?"

Daniel nodded and went to retrieve the coat. Cal was halfway to the back door. Leo followed.

Cal walked at a fast clip, and it took Leo a second to catch up to him on the gravel path leading to the steps spilling out onto the beach.

"Hey, what's with all the hush-hush?" asked Leo, starting to shiver as the cold wind whipped through his collared shirt.

"They've got your house wired. We can't talk in there."

"Wait, who has my house wired?"

Cal walked faster. "I'll tell you as soon as we get as far away from your house as we can. The sound of the waves should mask any directional microphones."

"Cal, what the hell is going on?"

"They know you're helping us and they've been watching."

"Who?"

Cal didn't answer.

By the time they'd walked down onto the beach, the wind was blowing hard, kicking up stinging sand in their faces. There wasn't a soul on the beach in either direction. Cal kept walking toward the large breakers. Leo followed, shivering harder, hands tucked in his armpits.

Once they'd gotten five feet from the Atlantic, Cal finally turned, looking all around, making sure no one was close. Not even the other houses were visible, the fog laying a dull cover over the landscape. They were alone.

"Can you tell me what's going on now, Cal? Come on, I'm freezing out here."

Cal didn't seem to care, gazing out over the ocean, dark clouds obscuring the horizon and a storm blowing in overheard.

"Why did you do it?" asked Cal over the sound of the pounding surf.

"Do what?"

"Why did you help Dryburgh?"

Leo face hardened. "What are you talking about?"

"You know what I'm fucking talking about. The stocks. The debt play with Russia."

Cal could tell by the look on Leo's face that he knew he was caught. Neil had found it all. Once they tracked Dryburgh's actions, it had only been a matter of time before the trail led to Leo's firm. To cap it all off, Leo's dead head of security had left more than enough proof, including video and documentation that proved Martindale was the mastermind behind the plot. He'd even had the foresight to leave a letter with a summary of his boss's actions and the final thought that Martindale was onto him with the words, "I think he knows, and that's why I'm leaving this for someone to find."

"You think you're so fucking smart, Cal. You have no idea."

"Please tell me."

"The world isn't all about right and wrong anymore. There's a whole world of gray that most people never take a second to consider. Did you know that if we go on the same course we've been on, China will own us in less than twenty years? It's true. I've done the math. I've been on the committees. These fucking communists want to own us. They want to see us ground into the dirt and piss on our graves. Well, I'm not gonna sit back and let it happen."

"So you got in bed with Geoffrey Dryburgh and concocted this scheme with the Russians."

"It never would have happened if the old president hadn't left office. With Zimmer we had a real chance. Sure, he'd be the scapegoat, but that was the price we were willing to pay."

"It wasn't just him, Leo. There were a lot of others who were hurt, who were going to lose it all."

"You think I don't know that? You think I don't care? Well I fucking do, goddammit. I care so much that I'm willing to risk everything I have to see that my country doesn't fall into the hands of the Russians and the Chinese."

"What about the money you were set to make? You mean to tell me that wasn't part of it?"

That question rocked Leo back on his heels. "What… what money?"

"Your old security chief left some files in a safety deposit box. He was tracking you for almost a year. He had everything, the names of the companies you and Dryburgh manipulated, the politicians you coerced or paid off and the exact plan you were already in the process of implementing to short sell millions of seemingly random stocks and then buy up as many treasury bills as you could once the President's new plan was implemented. He even had a taped conversation of you and Dryburgh talking about how he would help you once he took over the presidency. Oh, and that doesn't even include the people you either had killed or were going to kill just to get your way. Are you saying that wasn't true?"

Leo smiled, the facade gone. "Okay. You got me. What do you want me to say? That I did it all for my country? That I didn't want to make a dime? I'm human, okay?"

"And what about the employee that you killed, your own head of security? How did you do it, Leo? Let me guess, you lured him to your place and—"

"He deserved what he got! I warned him not to go snooping, but he didn't listen."

"So you killed him."

"I could tell that he was getting antsy. He was going to tell someone," said Leo, his eyes still cold.

"So why did you call us? Did you even know my father?"

"I knew who he was. And it wasn't even my idea to call you, it was Dryburgh's. He said you were somehow tied to the president and that if—"

"You took an oath, to defend our country against all enemies, foreign and domestic."

"If you still believe that word-for-word, you're more naive than you look, Cal. Arrest me if you want, but you know the friends I keep. I'll be out before you can say Smedley Butler."

Leo laughed and turned to walk back to his house. A stupid thing to do. He didn't get three steps. Zimmer had told Cal on his way to Southampton to assess the situation and deal with it as he saw fit. See what Martindale had to say and either bring him in or seek an alternative.

No hesitation. Cal's arm was around Martindale's neck and pulling him toward the roiling surf. Struggling to free himself, Leo first pulled with his hands and then threw elbows back into Cal. It didn't slow the Marine, who took the ineffectual blows as his shoes entered the water, then his ankles, a wave finally crashing over and soaking them both. In the lull between two waves Cal made his move, letting go of his chokehold and whipping Leo around to face him, Cal's hands now gripping the man's neck, thumbs inserted on either side of Leo's Adam's apple. The two Marines stared at each other, one in fear, the other with unwavering determination.

"You should know this part, Leo. One of the first lessons you learn in boot camp. There's only one thing you can do with a traitor."

Leo's eyes bulged as Cal dove forward, plunging the billionaire under the waves, blasting the last shred of breath out of his lungs with the freezing salt water and Cal's two knees driving into Leo's chest. The struggle lasted less than a minute, but still Cal held, taking the pounding of the relentless waves as they crashed in one after another. Finally, when he was certain Leo couldn't possibly be alive, Cal dragged the body deeper into the ocean, looking for the current he knew to be there. And then he found it, the undertow so strong that it almost swept him with it. Cal released the body and felt the tide take hold without prompting.

He turned back toward the house and moved to join Daniel who stood waiting with a towel on the beach. They had a plane to catch.

CHAPTER 50

The fog rolled over the rises and into the valleys without a sound, like a white carpet being put into place by an unseen hand. There wasn't a sound except for the drip of still-melting snow falling from the end of the roof and into a small puddle. Geoffrey Dryburgh loved those mornings, fresh cool air, the same his ancestors had probably felt years ago in the hills of the old country. Men and women carving out simple lives, oppressed by the Lords of Britain, struggling just to stay alive. He had more than they ever had, won by hard work and perseverance.

His thoughts were interrupted by thumping steps on the old wood floors, originally installed in the late 1800s. The front door squeaked open and Igor Bukov stepped out holding two steaming cups of coffee, their aroma quickly making their way to Dryburgh's senses. Dark roast, black as night.

"Here you are, Geoffrey." Bukov handed the first mug to his friend, who took it gratefully, inhaling deeply over the offering. He'd invited Dryburgh up for the day, no security. It had seemed like a strange request, but Dryburgh understood his friend's current predicament. The Russian President was not happy with his ambassador. Bukov had called in the middle of the night and asked for his help in containing the situation, and possibly helping him hide if needed. It wasn't the first time they'd met outside official channels.

"Nothing beats a cup of coffee on a morning like this."

Bukov chuckled. "While that may be true in America, in my country we tend to start cold days with a mug of vodka."

Dryburgh smiled, having spent more than a few of those early wake ups with his friend in some God-forsaken land, miles away from civilization.

"I like your place," said Dryburgh, sipping his coffee and enjoying the welcome warmth flowing through his body.

"It reminded me of one of my family estates in Russia. I bought it from an old farmer who could no longer maintain the land."

"Would you ever sell it?" Dryburgh was always on the lookout for good property. Land meant more to immigrants than the gold it was bought with, a lesson his father taught a young Geoffrey almost daily.

"If I was offered the right price…possibly."

Dryburgh returned his gaze to the pastures as Bukov took a seat in the Adirondack chair next to him. "So, what was so important that I had to drive all the way to Manassas?"

Bukov sighed. "This business with your president, it has my government very worried."

"As well they should be! Old Zimmer really called your bluff!"

"Geoffrey, it was you who told me that the President would have a very different reaction. Now I am the one being blamed for this mistake as the entire world comes down on my people."

It was true. The last two days had not been good for the Russians. Banks from Japan to Switzerland were threatening to freeze all Russian assets until the debacle was concluded. Every ally the Russians made in their planning went back on their word, their leaders personally calling the American president to apologize and seek to form bonds more solid than before. As far as the world was concerned, Russia was the leper no one wanted to touch. Even everyday Russians were clamoring for their once popular president to pull back and rescind the threat.

"I'm sorry it happened that way, but this isn't over yet. I still have a couple things up my sleeve. Trust me, by the end of the month, Zimmer and Southgate will be out, and I'll be in."

"Tell me what you plan to do."

Dryburgh told him.

Bukov nodded. "It sounds like you have things under control."

"You're goddamn right I do."

Bukov stood and looked out over his fields. "I think I may take a walk to think about what you've said. Do you have time to come?"

Dryburgh looked up at his friend and shrugged. "Sure, why not."

As he rose to join Bukov, he went to set his coffee on the arm of the white chair. Just as the mug touched wood, his hand disappeared, followed by the most blinding pain Dryburgh had ever felt. He held the stump as it gushed blood, geyser-like. Pitifully, he looked to his Russian friend, who was by now down the four steps standing on the brick path leading to the fence.

"I'm sorry, my friend," said Bukov. He turned and continued on his way, leaving Dryburgh on the porch, his lifeblood splattering onto the creaking wood slats.

The last thing Dryburgh would know was looking out to the foggy fields. The next second his head exploded like a watermelon from the supersonic .50 caliber round screaming for his life.

Bukov kept walking, breathing in the cool moist air, not an ounce of remorse on his conscience. He would be granted asylum in exchange for telling the Americans everything he could about Russia. It could take years. Meanwhile, he would live a very comfortable life in the United States.

Two figures emerged from the hillside, as if coalescing out of the mist. Ghosts. They took their time as they made their way down to Bukov.

Cal and Daniel met him by the old watershed, bricks crumbling from neglect, icicles still clinging to its edges like sad daggers used for the last time.

Daniel was carrying his Barrett sniper rifle and Cal had the weapon's accessory bag slung over his shoulder. Both Marines were wearing jeans and black t-shirts. There hadn't been much need for camouflage.

"You okay?" asked Cal.

"I'm fine, thank you," answered Bukov.

"Good. Daniel, you take care of the house and I'll get the ambassador to the car. The debriefing team is waiting."

Less than ten minutes later, the three men drove down the worn dirt path, the rising flames of centuries old wood filling their rearview mirror.

EPILOGUE

The smell of paperwork made Cal want to take a flame thrower to his entire desk. No matter how much he did, there always seemed to be more. His once tidy office was covered in mounds of files and reports. It wasn't even noon and Cal already had four paper coffee cups stacked in his trashcan.

It had only been a week since they'd wrapped up things with the President, but to Cal and his endless supply of admin work, it felt like a lifetime. Unfortunately, with the world back on the mend, he didn't have an excuse to avoid his office.

The Russians had finally caved and the President's bold initiative was scrapped. In exchange, the Russians and their cohorts had agreed to severe penalties, each assenting to give the United States five years without having to pay a penny of interest on their debt. Further, the guilty countries would have to pay an extra tax on top of any future investments they made with the U.S. It was a hefty price to pay, but much better than the alternative of having the world's financial markets go into a free fall.

With Travis now permanently in Washington, and Zimmer and Southgate on the same page, there wasn't much Cal could do except return to the task of helping SSI's new CEO, Marge Haines, get the company more business. He'd offered to be part of the team to debrief Igor Bukov, but the CIA had whisked the man away as soon as Cal and Daniel had dropped the former ambassador at the CIA safe house in Manassas.

Cal huffed for the umpteenth time that day, wishing he could delegate the mundane tasks of his position to someone else. Just as he reached for another inch-thick file, Marge Haines stepped into his office.

"And to what do I owe the pleasure of your presence, milady?" asked Cal, happy for the distraction.

"We need to talk."

Cal searched Marge's face, trying to read her expression. Nothing.

"Okay. What's up?"

"Not here. Let's go to my office."

"Hold on. If I'm about to get a scolding, I'd rather do it in here."

Marge stared at him with those lawyer eyes, accustomed to breaking lesser men. "Fine. If that's what you want."

"It is. Now, by the way you stormed in here I'm assuming it's something I did, although I can't imagine what that could be."

"I've been analyzing how SSI is doing business, and I think we need to make a few changes."

Cal flew out of his chair. "And what the hell is that supposed to mean? This is *my* company remember?"

Marge's face softened. "Look, I'm just doing what should've been done a long time ago."

"And what would that be?" Cal couldn't believe what he was hearing. He thought Marge was a friend, someone who believed in the company his father had started, that his cousin had grown, that the hard working employees called home. Now she was looking to take apart the well-oiled machine? It was total bullshit!

"Cal, I agree with everything you've done over the last couple years, but it's getting to the point where we can't hide it anymore. We're getting too big. Something will leak out eventually. It almost has before. We need to make a change."

Cal wanted to scream at the top of his lungs and tell Marge to go to hell. He and his men worked hard every single day to protect not only their company, but their country.

"Why don't you just spit it out, Marge. I'm not very good with riddles."

Marge nodded solemnly. "I'm sorry, Cal, but I think it's time for you to leave SSI."